William was really strange. He was chubby and he had a face like a grandpa, not the sort of kid that the guys would usually like, and yet he was taking over. He seemed right in the middle of things all of a sudden, with his little blue shirt buttoned right up to the neck.

Nutty even found himself sort of liking William in a way—weird as he was—and at the same time thinking there was something about William that was almost scary. He could outsmart a grown-up any day!

NUTTY FOR PRESIDENT

NUTTY
FOR
PRESIDENT

Dean Hughes

A BANTAM SKYLARK BOOK®
TORONTO · NEW YORK · LONDON · SYDNEY · AUCKLAND

RL 5, 008–012

NUTTY FOR PRESIDENT

*A Bantam Book / published by arrangement with
Atheneum Publishers, Inc.*

PRINTING HISTORY

*Atheneum edition published January 1981
2nd printing . . . September 1981
3rd printing . . . November 1982
A selection of the Weekly Reader Children's Book Club, September 1983
Bantam Skylark edition / March 1986
Skylark Books is a registered trademark of Bantam Books, Inc.
Registered in U.S. Patent and Trademark Office and elsewhere.*

*Bantam Books are published by Bantam Books, Inc. Its trade-
mark, consisting of the words "Bantam Books" and the por-
trayal of a rooster, is Registered in U.S. Patent and Trademark
Office and in other countries. Marca Registrada. Bantam
Books, Inc., 666 Fifth Avenue, New York, New York 10103.*

PRINTED IN THE UNITED STATES OF AMERICA

CW   0 9 8 7 6 5 4 3 2 1

For my son, Tom

CHAPTER ONE

"Let me say, first, that I am not a nurd. Unfortunately, your initial impression of me, in all probability, is that I am one. I believe, however, that I will soon dispel any such notion."

"Nutty" Nutsell wouldn't have believed it if he hadn't heard it. Here was this kid sitting across the lunch table from him, a fifth-grader, ten years old like the rest of them, talking more like the guy on the evening news. And to tell the truth, he *had* thought the kid looked like a nurd. William Bilks was his name, and he was a new kid in the school. He was short and what you might call "plump," if you were being nice. His hair was all combed nice and neat, with a cute little wave in the front, and his shirt was buttoned right up to the top. If not a nurd, at least a "near-nurd," Nutty decided.

"The image I project, I realize, is that of the in-

1

trovert and the scholastic achiever—the kind of person children usually call a 'brain'—and while that is not exactly a false image, it is a limited one. I can actually serve you fellows in ways that you would not imagine. I plan to prove that, in the next few days, and thereby win your allegiance."

Nutty forked in a glob of pasty mashed potatoes from his lunchtray and then glanced at "Bilbo" Blackhurst, who was sitting next to William. Nutty and Bilbo both started to grin; they looked down at their trays to avoid laughing out loud. But Nutty finally put on a straight face long enough to ask, "So what do you plan to do for us?"

William sort of dabbed at his lips with his napkin and then wiped his fingers, one at a time, as if he were polishing his mother's best silver spoons. "Well, first of all, I could . . . excuse me, but do people actually refer to you as 'Nutty'? Is there no other name I could—"

Richie Fetzer broke in. "His name is Frederick. You can call him that."

Nutty turned and punched Richie on the shoulder. "Shut up, Richie." Then he said to William, "'Nutty' is okay. You can call me that."

"Well, Nutty," (he pronounced it "nut-tea") "allow me to explain some of my background; that should facilitate your understanding. But first, could you oblige me by introducing everyone? I heard Mrs. Smiley call the roll, but I did not want to twist in my seat to determine which pupils were answering to the respective names called."

Nutty actually had to hold his breath for a second and not look at anyone. Even then, he almost broke out laughing. But finally he answered. "Okay, you know me. This *gentleman* wearing the baseball cap is Jimmy Ortega. His name is really Orlando Jiminez Ortega—that's how he says it, 'Him-in-ez'—but we thought it looked more like Jimmy-nez, so we started calling him Jimmy."

William Bilks reached across the table. For a second or two Orlando couldn't figure out what he wanted; but then he realized, and the two of them shook hands. Nutty had to duck his head again. He was almost ready to give up and just laugh right out loud.

"Do you approve of my calling you 'Jimmy'?" William asked.

"I guess so. It's okay. But I like my real name better. I was named after Orlando Cepeda."

"You must be a baseball fan," William said, sounding sort of happy about the idea.

"Sure. So's my dad."

"Yah," Nutty put in, "Jimmy knows everything about baseball."

"Wonderful," William said. "I am rather inclined toward baseball myself. I too have stored away a few facts—at least enough to make intelligent conversation."

"Is that right?" Orlando said. He was not very big for his age, but suddenly he sat up tall in his seat. "Who has the all-time record, in the majors, for stolen bases?"

"Well, of course, that's an easy one. Lou Brock took that one away from Ty Cobb a few years ago."

"What about strikeouts in a single game?"

"Sandy Koufax, as I recall."

"Lifetime home runs by a left-handed pitcher?"

"Oh, dear me. I really could not say. That could be Sandy Koufax again. Or perhaps. . . ."

"Babe Ruth," Orlando said, laughing. "He started out as a left-handed pitcher."

"Now that was a trick, you know. Very deceptive of you." Old William was chuckling away and nodding his head like somebody's grandpa. "Well, in any case, you do know your baseball, it seems."

"So do you," Orlando said, and then he stuck out *his* hand, and the two had themselves another handshake. Nutty about hit the deck.

"But shall I call you Jimmy or Orlando?" William wanted to know.

"You might as well call me Jimmy—to keep things straight—since all the other guys call me that."

"But Jimmy seems a terrible distortion of your given name. How about it, fellows? Couldn't we all call him Orlando? Since he prefers it?"

Richie started nodding, and so did Bilbo, and then even Nutty did, to his own surprise. Something weird was happening!

"Excellent," William said, "and now, who is this?"

"That's Charley Blackhurst, but we call him 'Bilbo' because he always talks about *The Hobbit*."

"Ah, a literary man," William said. "A man after my own heart. I too have spent many golden hours reading Tolkien. I try to read the *Lord of the Rings* trilogy once a year or so, when I get time on a weekend."

"On a weekend?" Bilbo said, as William grabbed his hand and started to pump it up and down. Bilbo seemed impressed.

"And this is Richie, did you say?" William asked, turning to his other side.

"Yuh. Richie Fetzer." Again there was a big old handshake. William seemed right in the middle of things all of a sudden, with his little blue shirt on—or maybe it was gray—buttoned right up around the neck, and the two little owls stitched on the pocket. It was the sort of thing your Aunt Gladys from Nebraska sends you in the mail for your birthday and you hide the same night and your mother is always asking whatever happened to it. This William was really strange. He was chubby and he had a face like a grandpa, just not the sort of kid that any of the guys would usually like, and yet he was taking over. Nutty even found himself sort of liking him in a way—weird as he was—and at the same time thinking there was something about William that was almost scary. It was like making friends with some grown-up—a teacher, or even a principal.

"His name is really Garth," Nutty said, grinning.

"Shut up," Richie said. But he was smiling too. Richie was a sort of funny-looking kid with big ears and hardly any eyebrows.

"He didn't like his name, so we thought up a new one for him. His mother comes to get him after school in a big old Mark V, so we decided he must be rich, and we started calling him Richie."

"That's a strange sort of—"

"It's okay," Richie said. "We're not rich really, but I like Richie for a name. Would you mind if we don't change it back to Garth?"

Nutty couldn't believe his ears. Richie didn't have to ask a thing like that from this overstuffed little kid. What was going on?

"So what should we call William, you guys?" Nutty asked. "I think William sounds a little too—"

"Actually, Nutty, I have given the subject some thought. I recognize that William is rather formal in sound; other children sometimes respond rather negatively to it. But Bill Bilks, or Billy Bilks, is terrible, and Will or Willy Bilks is no better. So all in all, William seems the best I can do."

"I don't know. We could call you Nurdo. Nurdo Bilks sounds pretty good doesn't it?" Nutty looked at the other guys for their reaction, but none of them would even look him in the eye.

"Come on, Nutty," Orlando said, "lay off."

Nutty could hardly believe what was happening!

"Actually, Nutty, that brings us back to our original topic. I don't mind your good-natured needling, but I assure you again that I am not what I may appear. Let me explain some things about myself. Whether for good or for ill, fate has granted me an extremely high I.Q. I suppose the term most people would use for me is 'child genius'—although I rather dislike the image attached to the term. In any case, I was offered a chance to enroll at the university this fall. I have read enough child psychology, however, to know that for a ten-year-old such a change could be damaging. I need to have a child's experiences; I need to have friends in my own peer group. So I talked things over with my father. I have been attending a nearby grammar school, but it had become clear to us that some other arrangement would be necessary. Our decision was to move me here to the university laboratory school. This seemed the right sort of environment for me, what with the library available, lectures and that sort of thing. Later in the year I may take a college course or two here on campus, but for now I want to fit in with you fellows as much as I possibly can."

Nutty looked around at the others. They were all staring at William as if he had just announced that he was an astronaut who had recently come back from outer space. And furthermore, they looked as if they believed him.

"Now I know that I am different," William went on. "That is both my blessing and my curse. But I believe that if I prove my worth to you, you will come to accept me."

"What do you mean, *worth*?" Nutty asked. He was really starting to get ticked off now.

"Nutty, I sense that you are annoyed with me. Give me a chance, will you please?"

Nutty didn't want to give him anything, but he couldn't think of what to say.

"One of the problems with being ten is that a person is relatively powerless. Almost everyone feels the right to direct the affairs of people our age. But I have found that knowledge gives one power. Authorities, accustomed to dealing with docile children, suddenly back down when they are faced with someone who knows what he is talking about and who is not frightened by adult intimidation. Let's say that there is something that you, as an entire group of fifth-graders, would like to have. Teachers simply say 'no' to most everything. But I have found that if I research the entire matter, demonstrate the feasibility of the plan in specific terms, back up the plan with logic and authoritative opinion, and show the teacher's own ignorance on the subject, he or she will capitulate every time. Principals are just the same."

"Hey, what about our fifth-grade field trip?" Bilbo said. "We wanted to go to Chicago, and Mrs. Smiley said it was too far. We asked her about it before school this morning."

"Great," William said. "I guarantee that you will make that trip this year. How about in the spring when the weather is nice?"

"But how can you? . . ."

"Just consider it done. I'll take care of it. But there are other things I can do. Let's suppose that one of you gets in trouble with the principal. I have read enough about education and the law to back down an average elementary school principal in minutes."

The other boys all began to smile, but Nutty said, "Not Dr. Dunlop."

"I have met Dr. Dunlop," William said. "Rather a

typical sort, with nothing more than a doctorate in education. He will be no problem whatsoever."

"Hey, this guy could come in handy," Richie said. He gave William a friendly nudge with his elbow. William grinned in his old-timer's way, with his forehead all wrinkled up and his head bobbing up and down.

Nutty was getting downright worried. "William, you talk big, but I'll believe it when I see it. It's fine to say what you'll do next spring. What can you do for us right now?"

"Well, let's see. Do you have a student council or student body officers?"

"Sure. We have a council and a president of the council."

"When is the election?"

"Next week, or maybe the week after that."

"Do all the students vote for the student council president, or just the members of the council?"

"Everybody does—except kindergarten."

"Good. How would you like to be the president, Nutty?"

"You gotta be kidding."

"No. Not at all."

Nutty looked at William for a minute; he was the kind of guy you had to be suspicious of, but it would be fun to be president. There wasn't much chance of that, though. "Look, I'm not even in the sixth grade," he finally said.

"Do the bylaws of the council say that the president must be in the sixth grade?"

"I don't know. But it's always a sixth-grader."

"I suspect we can get around that easily enough."

"You're crazy, William. Even if I could be nominated, I would never win. I mean *never*."

"Why not?"

"Why not? William, you don't know . . . I mean . . . well, for one thing, there are only fifteen in the fifth grade, and ten of them are girls. So that means we have five votes right here—if we have that many—and these are the only people in this whole school who would vote for me."

"Why?"

"The rest just wouldn't. Would they, Bilbo?"

"Well, I. . . ."

"Wait a minute," William said. "You are looking at this all wrong. Trust me. I know campaign strategy. I have done extensive reading on the subject. We can talk about image projection and grass-roots organizations and all that sort of thing later."

"William, I still say you're crazy," Nutty said. "I don't want to be president. It's the last thing in the world I want to do. Besides, there's this guy in sixth grade named Jim Hobble. He's the big wheel in everything. He's going to win. No one has a chance against him."

"Is he the good-athlete, piano-player, star-of-the-school-play type?"

"Exactly," Nutty said, and the others nodded.

"Kids don't actually like him, do they?"

"Like him?"

"Nobody likes him," Orlando said. "He thinks he's a big shot."

"Just as I thought," William said. "This will be child's play. Nutty, you will be the people's candidate, the common man. We don't have a lot of time before the election, so we will have to get to work on your image. How about tonight after school? Can you all gather for a short planning session right after school?"

They all thought they could, though Nutty felt he had to keep saying that he wasn't interested, that William was crazy. All the same, he didn't say that he wouldn't come, and inside he knew he would. The thought of beating Jim Hobble was too fantastic. How sweet it would be to beat that big jerk. But the whole idea was stupid. William would never be able to pull it off.

CHAPTER TWO

All afternoon Nutty's mind kept wandering back to the thought of being president of the school. In a way, it scared him. He didn't know how to do that kind of stuff. All the same, he couldn't help liking the idea. He hadn't ever done anything important—anything to make people think he was *somebody*. His parents were always telling him, "Freddy, you've got to be a little more aggressive—show what you can do. You'll never get anywhere if you just sit back and let everyone else hog the spotlight." Nutty always let that kind of stuff run right off his back—or at least he thought he did. But being president was the kind of thing that would make his mom and dad proud of him. Maybe for once somebody around the house besides his ballet-dancing, cutie-pie sister would get some attention. But the whole idea was still stupid. No one would vote for him.

Mrs. Smiley was bubbling all over the place today, but Nutty hardly paid any attention. She was still in that "Oh, this is the first day, so let's get off to a great start" mood. She would get over it in a few days, and then everything would settle into the usual grind. It was a little school, and the kids knew all the teachers. The story on Mrs. Smiley was that she was always trying to "get next to you," like she was your big sister or something. She was young and kind of pretty. When Nutty's mother saw her, she said Mrs. Smiley was "striking." Nutty thought she was a strikeout.

But now she was saying, "I want you all to take out a sheet of paper and begin writing an essay. You have half an hour; if you don't finish, please complete the assignment this evening."

Homework already!

Mrs. Smiley walked away from the blackboard, toward the desks at the front of the room. (Nutty was as far to the back as he could get.) "Now I don't want to make you do one of those 'what I did for summer vacation' papers. I want this to be *fun*." Her eyes began to dart around, and Nutty knew that something bad was coming. "Imagine you are an animal—a duck, or a giraffe, or a yak, or a lizard—anything you like. Now. What are you thinking? What is going through your animal head? Put yourself into this. Be *creative*. Let's have some *great* papers."

Orlando leaned across from his desk and said, "I told you what she was like—just like my sister said."

"This could be a long year," Nutty whispered back to Orlando.

"Mrs. Smiley." It was Mindy—sweet little Mindy Marshall. She had her hand up. She always had her hand up.

"Yes? Is it Melinda?"

"You can call me Mindy. All my friends do."

"Fine. What is it, Mindy?"

"Would it be all right if I'm a little squirrel?"

"Yes, of course. That's a wonderful idea." Mrs. Smiley flashed her sparkly teeth.

But Nutty leaned over and said, "No Mindy, you're supposed to be something other than yourself."

Mindy spun around and shot back, "Cute, Nutty, really cute. That means you can't be an ape, I guess."

Nutty thought about some comebacks but decided not to use them. Mrs. Smiley was giving him the "now let's not get that started" look. Nutty knew *that* look. He knew the whole routine. He suspected this would be another year like all the rest. Soon Mrs. Smiley would decorate the room with cute little autumn leaves—orange and red and gold—cut from construction paper. And then it would be pumpkins and black cats, and right after that Pilgrims. Then the snowmen and Santa Clauses would come out, right about the time practice began for the Christmas program. Mindy would be saying, "Since the program is 'Christmas in Many Lands,' could we do 'Christmas in Hawaii'? My family went there last year for vacation and I got this grass skirt and I could be. . . ." Mrs. Smiley would say, "Wonderful, Mindy," and that would be that. Then out would come the valentines, and then the spring blossoms, and finally there would be just tired, empty walls for a while, until it all ended again.

"I'm going to be a slug," Orlando whispered.

Nutty turned and gave him a long look. "Congratulations," he finally said. Maybe he *would* run for president. It was better than nothing.

That afternoon at three o'clock, when the bell rang, William got hold of Nutty immediately. "Listen, Nutty, why don't you tell the others we'll meet in ten minutes. I need to have you come with me."

Where did William get the idea that he was the boss? But there was no time to argue. Nutty told the other boys where to meet and hurried down the hallway, just a little behind William. William sort of waddled, but he walked pretty fast, taking three steps while Nutty was taking two. Nutty was a lot taller than William. And it occurred to him that he must be crazy, following that little shrimp around. A couple of fourth-grade boys even stopped to watch them go by. They might have said something, but Nutty shot them a dirty look and they didn't make any cracks.

William marched right into the principal's office and stepped up to the secretary's desk. Nutty stood back, close to the door. He had no idea they had been coming here, of all places. What was going on! Could the kid be a dwarf and a spy for Dr. Dunlop? Was he going to turn him in for saying the lunch looked like puke?

"I would like to see Dr. Dunlop on a matter of some urgency," William said.

The secretary was a thin, pale woman, with black eyes that reminded Nutty of balls of lead. She looked sort of surprised. "Could you tell me what business. . . ." Her voice just sort of died out. She must have realized she was saying to a kid what she normally only said to adults.

"I believe it would be better if I explained my business directly to the principal," William said.

She nodded. She stood up. And then she stopped, as if maybe she was thinking things over. Finally she walked from the room. Nutty gave serious thought to taking off, but he was curious to see what William was up to. In a few seconds the secretary came back. "Dr. Dunlop will see you now." William turned, motioned to Nutty, then walked toward the office door. Nutty wanted to turn and leave, and he almost did, but for some reason he followed William into the office.

Dunlop did not get up; he just looked over the top of his bifocals and said, "Yes?" He was a hefty man with dark, fat cheeks, and though he wasn't quite bald, he was awfully thin on top.

"Dr. Dunlop," William began, taking a seat and motioning for Nutty to do the same, "I would like to see a copy of the constitution and bylaws for the student council, if you don't mind."

Dunlop just kept staring at William. Nutty wondered for a minute if Dunlop was even listening. But finally he said, "I don't believe we have ever written anything up . . . formally, that is. We simply. . . ."

"Just as I suspected," William said. "Perhaps I can write such a document later this year, if the council wishes my help. But for now, perhaps you can explain your policies, which apparently, for the present, derive authority only from precedence."

"Well, yes . . . yes . . . I suppose . . . yes, precedence."

"Is it mandatory that the student body president be a member of the sixth grade?" William asked. Nutty thought William sounded like one of those lawyers on television who always walks back and forth and takes off his glasses when he talks. Dr. Dunlop was starting to play with a pencil on his desk.

"Well, Mr. Bilks—or, I mean, William—we have always felt that the sixth-grader was naturally more suited to a . . . position . . . of such . . . how should I say? . . . of such . . . a. . . ."

"Sir, when you say 'we,' do you mean the administration or the students?"

Old Dunlop cleared his throat. He sounded as if he was about to choke. "Well, I suppose all . . . that is, both . . . have felt more or less it would be . . . you know . . . the best thing for everybody . . . I suppose."

"So you would not characterize this as a hard and fast rule, but merely a tradition?"

"Yes, William—that's the idea."

"Then, should a member of another grade run for office, this would not actually break any rule?"

Dr. Dunlop waited. He looked like the defendants always do on TV—the ones who get caught in the lawyer's trap. He started drumming a pencil on his desk and looking at it as if it were the most interesting pencil he had ever seen. "William, we have always asked the sixth-graders to nominate two or three of their students and then we. . . ."

"Ah—then you *have* discriminated against the younger students, in effect, by not opening up the nominations to a fully democratic procedure."

"Now, Mr. Bilks, that is a very harsh way to put it. This is a grade school, not the national government. We certainly had no intention to . . . I mean, by all means . . . we have every desire to do what is . . . fair . . . of course." He stopped for a second, and then he seemed to get some of his confidence back. Just as William was about to say something again, Dr. Dunlop said, "Consider, young man, now that I think about it, even the constitution of this great country. A man under thirty . . . a . . ."

"Thirty-five, sir."

"Yes, thank you. A man under thirty-five cannot run for president. This is not meant to. . . ."

"I understand that concept, sir. I would certainly agree that a kindergartener, for instance, would not be prepared to guide our school. But you are implying, if I understand you correctly, that only a person in the top one-seventh age grouping is qualified to serve. By that logic the American government would have to set the qualifying age for presidential candidacy at sixty or higher, which would hardly do. The point is to avoid the person who is too young and in-experienced, not to have rule by the senior citizen."

"Now, I don't mean that. . . ."

"And besides, Dr. Dunlop, you have no constitution or bylaws that set out your stipulations. You only informally create rules as you go, privately inviting only one group to participate in the nominations."

"Now, Mr. Bilks, let me remind you again that this is not the government of the United States; this is an elementary. . . ."

"You were the one who suggested the comparison."

Nutty noticed that Dunlop's neck, down below the dark line where his shaven beard left off, had turned all red and splotchy. He noticed too that William's feet just barely reached the floor when he sat up straight in his chair. Something about the combination of those two observations made him duck his head to keep from laughing.

Dunlop didn't say anything this time, and William let him stew. "What exactly, Mr. Bilks—William—did you have in mind?" he finally asked. "What is it you want?"

"Oh, I want nothing, sir. I was just thinking . . . in lieu of a constitution—which I can help write up later, as I suggested—why don't we, for now, open up the nominations to the three top grades? You could simply announce that petitions with, say, ten names must be submitted to your office by a certain date, perhaps two weeks from the announcement. Chances are a sixth-grader will win, but the democratic process will be allowed, any hint of discrimination ended, and all should be happy."

"Why, yes, William, that sounds fair enough. I certainly want to be . . . a . . . democratic . . . and all that sort of thing. We could do as you suggest, I suppose."

"Excellent. Thank you, sir." William stood up and put his hand out toward Dr. Dunlop. For a minute the principal stared at William's chubby little paw; then he took it, gave it one quick shake, and let go of it as if it were hot. William turned and started toward the door, but Nutty got there ahead of him.

"A . . . a . . . Mr. . . . a . . . William."

The boys stopped and looked back. "Yes, sir?"

"What exactly is it that you are trying to . . . a . . . do?"

"Do, sir?"

"Yes. I mean, do you plan to run for president?"

"Oh, no, sir. Never. I'm not the type."

"I see. Frederick, are you involved in this?"

"In what, sir?"

"Why is it that you came along?"

"Because William asked me to."

"I see." He looked at the boys, lowering his head because of his bifocals. "William, when you and your father came by to speak to me about your coming here, I was assured that you would be no special . . . a. . . ."

"Problem, sir?" Dunlop nodded. "Am I a problem, sir?"

"Oh no, I simply. . . ."

"Good. Thank you, Dr. Dunlop. Good day, sir." The boys left. They headed back down the hallway, Nutty almost running to keep up.

"Wow, William, you were great. Unbelievable. I never say anything like that."

"Thanks, Nutty; nice of you to say so. Fact is, however, my logic was full of holes. I am rather embarrassed to have been reduced to such sophism, but we got what we wanted. Right?"

"Right," Nutty said, but he felt very strange. He had liked watching old Dunlop squirm, but still, something about it bothered him. If he had just walked in and socked Dunlop in the nose and Dunlop had smiled and said, "Thank you, Frederick," Nutty wouldn't have felt a whole lot different from the way he felt now.

"Where are the other boys?" William asked.

"Out in the back by the swings."

"By the *swings*?"

"Well, you know. It was just the first place I happened to think of."

It turned out that Richie had not been able to stay, but Orlando and Bilbo were out there, each sitting in a swing, but not swinging. "All right, fellows," William said, as he walked up to them, "we need to get organized. Dunlop just caved in, as I assumed he would. We can get Nutty on the ballot by collecting ten names. There is no problem on that, of course. We'll worry about that a little later. Why don't we. . . ."

"Ah . . . William."

"Yes, Nutty. What is it?"

Cripes, that little jerk even sounded like a crumby teacher. He might be able to handle adults that way, but kids are smarter. "It may not be so easy as you think—getting ten names, I mean. I can probably force my little sister to sign, and there's this kid in my neighborhood who might if I. . . ."

"No, Nutty, that won't do—not at all. How could we count on them when it came to a secret ballot? We must create the right sort of image for you. The students must *want* to vote for you."

"You got a big job ahead of you, William," Orlando said.

"Why, Orlando? What sort of image does Nutty have now?"

"You mean, what do the kids think of him?"

William nodded. "That's right."

Orlando pushed the swing back a little bit and then let it rock forward. He seemed to be thinking, but at the same time a smile was beginning to show up in his dark eyes and in the corners of his mouth. "Well, okay. First, almost everyone in the school knows him. But mainly they know him because he likes to joke around a lot, and he's always making wisecracks in the cafeteria or at recess. Even in class. He's sort of funny sometimes, but usually he thinks he's a whole lot funnier than he is."

"Hey!" Nutty said, and he reached out and gave Orlando a push on the chest. Orlando just let the swing ride back, and he smiled at Nutty. Nutty couldn't believe it. Orlando was getting pretty darn brave in his old age. "I notice you laugh plenty at the things I say," Nutty said.

"Well, some of the things you do are so stupid they're kind of funny," Bilbo said; "like the time you set off that—"

"Shut up, Bilbo," Nutty said. "You don't have to bring that up."

"Nutty," William said with authority. "For a moment you be silent. We cannot have any skeletons in your closet that I don't know about. Go ahead, Bilbo, tell me about it."

And Nutty *was* silent, but he sure as heck didn't know why. He was not going to let this . . . this teacher, or whatever he was . . . someone's old maid aunt dressed up in a kid's body . . . boss him around this way. He wanted to pound the little nurd into the ground and then go to work on Orlando . . . *Jimmy* . . . and have Bilbo for dessert.

Bilbo got up from the other swing. Nutty tried to stare him down, but it didn't work. The creep even looked like a hobbit. Probably had hairy feet! It would serve him right to take off his shoes and expose the truth to the rest of the world.

"You ought to know about this thing he did, William," Bilbo said. "It's the one thing he's really famous for. He got hold of some firecrackers last year."

"Bilbo, you frog-face, lay off, will you?" Nutty said, but he was silenced again when William shot him a dirty look.

Bilbo went on, "I think a cousin of his sold them to him. Most of the firecrackers were just little things,

but he had this one big round one they call a cherry
bomb. Well, Nutty decided he was going to set it off at
school. He was going to light it in the boys' room, then
step out and chuck it down the hallway and then jump
back in."

"Yuh, and who dared me to do it?" Nutty said.

"Well," Bilbo answered, "Nutty thought up the
idea, but we didn't think he would do it. We dared
him, but we didn't think he would be stupid enough
to actually. . . ."

"Look," Nutty said, stepping toward Bilbo.
"Don't call me stupid unless you want your nose
parted down the middle."

"For the last time, Nutty," William said, "hold
your tongue and let me hear the whole story."

Nutty spun around. "I'll tell you the *whole* story,
William. I lit the dumb thing and looked out to throw
it and the janitor was coming down the hall. So I ran
back in and threw it in a toilet and flushed it. How was
I supposed to know that cherry bombs will go off under water?"

Bilbo and Orlando both began to laugh. "You
should have seen it," Orlando said. "It blew holes in
the pipes all over the school. Water was running all
over the place. They had to send us home for the rest
of the day."

"That is, most of us," Bilbo said. "Nutty had to
stay and help clean up—and then he got expelled for
a week. Everybody in the whole school knew who did
it. I don't think many kids would think he was quite
the type to get elected president."

William shook his head sadly, and then he looked at Nutty.

"Okay," Nutty said. "I told you that you couldn't do it. Didn't I, nurdo? And that's fine with me. I don't want to be the stupid president anyway. It was all your idea. And Bilbo and Jimmy, you two are gonna pay for this."

"Hush, Nutty. Don't make things worse than they are."

"Listen, you little nurd." Nutty reached for William. And then suddenly William had him by the arm, and Nutty felt his body cartwheeling through the air. He ended up on his back looking up at William, who was standing over him with one foot on each side of his ribs.

"I know karate, Nutty, but I don't like to use it. Now listen to me. I said I would make you president of this school, and I will still do it. But it is going to be more difficult than I first realized. I need to do some serious analysis tonight. We'll confer at school tomorrow, and go on from there."

William walked away. Nutty was still staring at the sky.

CHAPTER THREE

The next morning when Nutty got to school, William was standing at the front door waiting. Richie and Bilbo were with him.

"Nutty, I need to talk to you," William said. There he was in his little blue jacket, zipped all the way to the neck. It was already warm that morning, and it was going to be hot before the day was over; no one else in the school would have a jacket on. Nutty felt like throwing an insult at William—maybe ask him if his mommy dressed him—but he didn't say anything.

"We have an uphill climb, Nutty. We have to get to work before the day is over."

"Listen, William, I'll make it easy on you. Just drop the whole thing, like I told you yesterday. See yuh around." He started to walk away.

"Wait a minute, Nutty. I'm sorry, but that just is

not possible now. I have set too many wheels in motion. Here comes Orlando. That's good. We're all here now. This group will head up the operation. Now listen. We don't have much time, but I can brief everyone on our initial progress." Orlando had said "Hi" somewhere in the middle of William's little speech, but it was ignored. "This is my theory: Nutty has two major liabilities—or let's see, how would you fellows say that?—two major problems. He is considered frivolous, and he is notorious for the one unfortunate incident with the firecracker."

"William, I told you that—"

"Don't interrupt, Nutty," William said, almost exactly the way Mrs. Smiley would have said it. Next William would probably start calling him Frederick.

Richie was trying not to laugh, but Orlando was cracking up. "That's what he is all right—friv-o-less. What does that mean, anyway, William?"

"Orlando, excuse me, but frivolous is what you are being right now."

"Wow, I didn't know I knew how."

Richie and Bilbo laughed, and even Nutty smiled, though he was still in a lousy mood. But William didn't seem to find Orlando very funny. "Now listen, everyone. This is important. Nutty, in a week you will be more popular than you ever thought possible, and then you will be glad you did not back out of this. Just trust me. I have taken the first steps to erase this image of . . . well, let's say silliness. We shall turn this apparent weakness into a strength. I called

the local newspaper last night. It runs a daily feature
on a local citizen. They call it 'Today's Neighbor.'"

"Oh yah, on the front page," Richie said. "They
always have somebody's picture and then a little story
about him."

"That's correct. I called last night and com-
plained ·'..at the newspaper had not featured enough
children lately. The reporter who does the story said
that was probably true, and so then I suggested Nutty.
I told him Nutty was an interesting young fellow who
plans to be a comedian when he grows up. This afternoon Nutty and I have an appointment for an inter-
view."

"Comedian! Me?"

"Of course. He'll write that up, and suddenly you
won't be just a nutty kid, but a future star. Kids have a
tendency to think that anything that makes the newspaper like that is a big thing."

"I have to go to the dentist this afternoon," Nutty
mumbled.

"Don't worry about that. I'll call and get you another appointment. What is your dentist's name?"

Nutty just stared at William for a few seconds.
"Vogel," he said, but then he added, "Oh never mind.
I'll call . . . I mean actually I don't have an appoint-
ment. I made that up."

"I thought so," William said. "That's why I called
your bluff. But let that be a lesson, Nutty. You must be
careful not to get trapped that way. Sometimes, in the
public interest, a politician must avoid telling the
whole truth, but you must never allow yourself to get

into a position where you can be caught as you just were."

Orlando was cracking up again. "Nutty, a politician. I can just see that. 'Hi, I'm Nutty Nutsell, an' I wanna be yer *pres*ident.'"

"Shut up, *Jimmy*," Nutty said, almost yelled.

"My name is *Orlando*."

"Now both of you stop it," William said, stepping between them. "And Nutty that is the last time you are going to speak to anyone—absolutely anyone—that way. All the image projection in the world will only backfire if you persist in your aggressive behavior. You and I are going to have to spend many hours together. I am going to coach you constantly until we put together a package we can sell to the people."

Orlando started to laugh again, and Nutty let him laugh. His problems were bigger than Orlando. He, Nutty, seemed to be caught in a whirlwind he couldn't escape. Of course he could just walk away, but William's authority, strange as it was, seemed too real. And besides, whether he wanted to admit it or not, he did like the idea of being president.

"Anyway, this newspaper thing will get you started, and then I will arrange for you to do a stand-up comedy routine somewhere soon—this will add credence to the press story. But the second problem is more critical and demands more dramatic measures to effect a reversal. Dunlop is holding an assembly in a few days. As I understand it, he always gets up and welcomes everyone back, and then explains a few of the school rules, and that sort of thing."

The boys were standing in a half-circle in front of William; they all nodded, and Richie said, "And then they always have some kind of dumb program—teachers singing and playing the piano and stuff like that."

"I see," William said. "What I plan—and I still have to refine my thinking on this—is a confrontation between Nutty and Dunlop. Nutty will challenge Dunlop on some rule or student privilege and will skillfully present the students' point of view before the entire student body. He will force Dunlop to back down—at least to some significant degree."

All the boys were grinning, except Nutty. Orlando said, "William, you better stick to reading books or inventing new machines or something. There's no way you're going to pull *that* off. Nutty will probably fill his pants if Dunlop even takes a long look at him."

Nutty knew he couldn't stand up to Dunlop—not in a million years—but he didn't want to hear *Jimmy* say it. But what good would it do to say anything? William was going to lead him right into disaster, and there was no way to stop it. Unless, of course, he could catch a freight train headed for China.

"Don't worry, Orlando," William said. "I will have Nutty thoroughly coached. I'll teach him exactly what to say. You won't believe it's the same old Nutty speaking. In fact, it won't be. Nutty is going to realize his potential in the next few weeks, and he will become a different human being. He will demonstrate to the entire school that he is a leader, not a mere goof-off."

What a hot shot that character thought he was! But again there didn't seem to be any point in saying anything. Besides William was busy explaining that grass-roots organizations would be set up, with class representatives in each grade. The fifth-grade boys would serve as the main staffers and direct the organization. For now, he said, no mention of Nutty's candidacy should be made, but the boys should begin to spread positive ideas about Nutty by telling people how much he had changed. And another idea should be planted everywhere: someone had to beat Jim Hobble.

For Nutty, the day was a long one. He couldn't concentrate on his schoolwork, because all he wanted to do was imagine creative ways to bump off old William. But William had taken over the desk next to him that morning. And when he finished his trigonometry, he took a look and saw that Nutty hadn't done any of his math problems. After checking to make sure Mrs. Smiley wasn't watching, he took Nutty's workbook and quickly did all the problems. But he sent back a note with the workbook: "Don't start to depend on such assistance. I will not provide it in the future. But I will tutor you in math after school. You need to get all your grades up. It is important that teachers start saying positive things about you in order to reinforce your new image. (Destroy this note immediately.)"

New image. NEW IMAGE. Nutty never wanted to hear those words again. But that afternoon, as he walked over to the newspaper office with William, he heard the words at least a dozen times. William told him what to say to the reporter, but he also told him

not to worry because he would step in if Nutty
couldn't handle the situation.

The reporter was young, maybe twenty-four or
-five. He had fairly long hair—red—and he was wearing jeans. This made Nutty a little less scared, but not
less enough.

"So you're the kid they call Nutty?" the reporter
said. "Sit down. And you must be William Bilks."
William nodded and stuck out his hand. The reporter
shook it and sort of chuckled as he sat down behind
the desk.

"William tells me you want to be a comedian."
Nutty nodded. "Is that why the kids call you Nutty?"
Another nod. "Should I put down Frederick, or Fred,
or do you prefer Nutty?"

"Nutty."

"Okay." The reporter looked at Nutty for a few
seconds. He was still smiling. "You're kind of quiet for
a comedian, aren't you?"

"He's actually not," William said. "When he gets
up before a crowd his entire manner changes. He's a
born performer and a true wit. Tell him that joke you
told me on the way over here, Nutty."

Nutty looked blank for a moment, and then he
brushed his hair away from his eyes and licked his lips.
"Did you hear about the kid who had training wheels
on his bike for five years?" Nutty's question had been
directed to the reporter, but no one would have
known it. He stared ahead, straight at the wall, and he
spoke just loud enough to be heard.

The reporter shook his head. "No," he said. "I didn't hear about that."

"Yuh, he just couldn't get them trained."

The reporter laughed, but apparently more at Nutty than at his joke. "Yup. A born performer. A true wit." Nutty gave some serious thought to climbing under his chair.

"Nutty has to have an audience," William said. "You cannot imagine the change that comes over him when he gets up before a big crowd."

"Yes, you mentioned that," the reporter said. "I'd like to see that. Nutty, where have you performed?"

William answered, "He does mostly just small-time gigs right now. You know, at school. In the cafeteria he entertains almost every day. Impromptu, spontaneous spots, mostly. He's tremendous at improvising his own materials."

"I'll bet he is. I'll *bet* he is."

Nutty wanted to scream at William to shut up. He wanted even more to zip William's little blue jacket right up over William's little blue head.

"Nutty, have you tried to model your comedy on the work of any particular comedian?"

"No," Nutty said.

"Well, actually," William said, "he's too modest to say so, but he has taken the best from several artists. He has the style in repartee of George Burns, the timing of Jack Benny, the sharpness of Don Rickles, and the zaniness of Steve Martin."

"What are you, William, his press agent?" the reporter asked.

"Oh, no. Just a friend and admirer. But Nutty is entirely too modest. He hates to talk about himself."

"Yah. I can see that." Nutty didn't miss the sarcasm.

"It's all a joke," Nutty thought about saying. "I dressed my grandpa up like a kid—just to see if we could get away with it. Here, I'll pull up his pant legs and show you his varicose veins." But instead, he sat there like a half-wit, and he hated himself for it.

"William," the reporter finally said, "what are you up to?"

"Up to, sir?"

"Yah. What's your gimmick. Why are you pushing this kid?"

"Just out of friendship, sir."

"Who are you, anyway? Are you really a kid?"

"Don't I look like one?"

"Not exactly."

William laughed. "I'm just a regulation kid. I suppose I do look different, somehow. You are not the first to comment to that effect."

"Well," the reporter said, after leaning back in his chair, "I guess I'll run this. All I need is a couple of paragraphs. We don't have to have any particular justification. We usually just pick people at random. But I think I ought to do a story on you, William. I think you would make a feature story."

"Oh no, sir. I don't do anything special. I'm the lab school nurd. Nutty calls me nurdo."

"I'll bet he does."

The reporter had to get Nutty's address, his parents' names, and that sort of thing. Nutty answered those questions for himself, quietly but accurately. Then the reporter walked with them to the front door. "Listen," he said, "we're going to need a picture. What if I send a photographer over to the school tomorrow. Maybe he can catch ol' Nutty in the middle of one of his famous impromptu, spontaneous-type gigs in the cafeteria."

"Oh no, I. . . ."

"That'll be perfect," William said. "He may be a little nervous under pressure, but he needs that experience. Our lunch starts at eleven-fifty. Why don't you have someone come at noon. We'll make sure something happens."

"Okay," the reporter said. He stuck his fingers into his jeans' pockets in front. "Nutty, you stick with ol' William. He's either going to make you a star or a nervous wreck—one of the two."

Nutty gave a stupid little nod. William said, "Thank you ever so much."

The boys walked a few strides down the sidewalk. William glanced back to see if the reporter was gone. "This has turned out better than I hoped. But don't ever let me down like that again, Nutty. Do you understand? We have a tremendous amount of work to do on you. It's going to take everything we have to get you that presidency."

CHAPTER FOUR

William showed up at Nutty's house that night before the dishes had even been cleared from the table. When the doorbell rang, Nutty's mother said, "Who could that be?" For some reason Nutty just hadn't been able to tell his family about William or about the election.

"I think it's a friend of mine," Nutty said.

"Charley Blackhurst?"

"No. A new guy." Nutty went to the door. His idea was to take William directly to his room and avoid all the explanations. But William had hardly gotten through the front door when Mrs. Nutsell came in from the kitchen and said, "Let's see. I don't believe I have met you before."

William was taking off his jacket. He finished the "procedure" without hurry, and then he draped the jacket over his arm. "Yes, ma'am, it is true, we have not met. I am William Bilks, and I presume I am correct in thinking that you are Mrs. Nutsell. Most happy to make your acquaintance."

Mrs. Nutsell was definitely surprised, maybe even a little flustered. "That's nice," she said. She began to turn, as though she would leave, and then she turned back. Nutty noticed that she patted her hair, as if she wanted to straighten it, but it wasn't messed up.

"You have an elegant home, Mrs. Nutsell. Have you lived here long?"

"Thank you, William. We've been here just over four years."

"Are you new to Missouri then?"

"Well, no. My husband and I are both from the St. Louis area, but we are new to this western side of the state." She was catching on—Nutty could see that—but she still looked confused. "Are you new here, William?"

"Oh my, no. My father is a chemist with the R and H Chemical Company here in town. He has been with them for years."

"Well, that's interesting. Fred—my husband—is with R and H himself. But he's in sales. I don't know whether he would know your father or not—it's such a big company. Half the town works there."

"I will certainly ask my father, Mrs. Nutsell." For a moment no one said anything, and Nutty was hoping to get William into his room without any more questions, but then William said, "I suppose you are all excited about the coming election."

"Election?"

"You mean Nutty hasn't told you that he is going to be the next school president?"

"School president?"

"Yes. I'm his campaign manager. I assure you, I am going to see to it that he wins."

Mrs. Nutsell put her hand on Nutty's shoulder. "Freddy, why didn't you tell me? That's wonderful. School president."

"It was William's idea. I doubt that I'll. . . ."

"Didn't he tell you that his picture is going to be in the newspaper either? He's becoming quite a local celebrity."

"Picture? No. Just a minute." Mrs. Nutsell stepped back to the opening that led to the living room. "Fred, come here a minute. I want you to hear this."

Nutty groaned. All he needed was for his father to get wind of this. He came to the door holding a newspaper that was unfolded and nearly dragging on the floor. He looked down at Nutty and then at William.

"Hello, sir. I'm William Bilks." William stuck out his hand, and Mr. Nutsell smiled a little but he shook hands. "Apparently your son has been keeping some very exciting news to himself. I'm afraid he is entirely too humble. He is running for president of the laboratory school at the university, and I am his campaign manager. I believe I can say with some degree of safety that you can expect him to win."

"Well. Is that so?" Mr. Nutsell folded the newspaper and stuck it under one arm. "Did you say your name was William?"

"Yes, sir."

"I don't believe I have met you before, William. Are you new to the school?"

"To the school, yes. But not to the community."

"And you say Freddy is going to win?"

"Yes, sir. He is a richly talented young man, and if I may say so, he has the best campaign manager he could get." William sort of chuckled at his own little joke.

"Fred," Mrs. Nutsell said, "his picture is going to be in the paper."

"Is that so?" Mr. Nutsell said, and he looked very pleased. "All the candidates, or just Freddy?"

"It's a special feature just on Nutty—as we friends all call him. It centers on his future in the comedy business."

"Comedy business?" Mr. Nutsell looked at Nutty, and Nutty sort of shrugged.

"Yes, Mr. Nutsell," William said. "Your son has a gift—the gift to raise spirits through the inspiration of laughter. I predict that he'll be famous for it some day—if he doesn't decide to pursue a career in politics instead. But for now, we are taking the first step by getting him elected president of the school."

Mrs. Nutsell adjusted her big round glasses. Nutty could tell she was trying to act natural, but he knew she was really excited about the whole thing. His father had rolled the newspaper into a little club and had started to drum with it against his leg. But now he raised it in the air and shook it a time or two, then pointed it at Nutty. "Freddy, this is good news—the best I've had in *quite some time*. It's what I've been telling you, isn't it?" He waited for Nutty to answer, but Nutty didn't. He couldn't remember his dad saying anything that had the slightest connection with elections or newpapers or anything else they had just been talking about. "I knew you had the stuff. I think you're going to be a Nutsell after all."

Nutty was wondering what it meant to be a Nutsell, after all, but he only said, "The picture is just going to be in that 'Today's Neighbor' thing they do every night."

Mr. Nutsell didn't listen. "Was it Bilks?" he asked.

"Yes, sir. William Bilks."

Mrs. Nutsell said, "Fred, William's father is at R and H. He's a chemist. Maybe you. . . ."

"I think I've heard the name," Mr. Nutsell said. "I'll have to drop over and say hello when I get a chance. Maybe we could have your parents over for dinner one of these evenings."

"That would be most pleasant," William said.

Everyone stood silent for a moment, and Nutty was about to make a dash for the bedroom, when Mr. Nutsell said, "Well, well. This is wonderful." He pointed the newspaper at William and said, "Let me know if I can help you. I'm in sales, you know. I just might have some ideas you could use. I'll let you two get to work now though. I guess you have planning to do. Awfully nice to meet you, William." Out came Mr.

Nutsell's hand, and he and William had another handshake. Nutty couldn't believe it.

Then finally they got to go to Nutty's room. But not before Nutty glanced back to see both of his parents still standing in the hall, talking and smiling. And suddenly it seemed that maybe it would be better to go back to letting his little sister get all the attention.

William had written up five jokes for Nutty. None of them sounded very good. But all that evening Nutty practiced them by telling them to William. Yet, even when he knew them so well he was sure he'd dream about them, he was scared he would forget everything when he got up in front of a bunch of people. But William told him that he was "pleased with his progress." "Now don't worry," he said as he left, "once you get up before those youngsters, the best will come out of you. You're a ham at heart."

Nutty hoped so. But by noon the next day he was too nervous to eat and too worried to hope. The fifth-grade boys were all sitting at their usual table. "Now don't worry," William told Nutty, "you'll be fine. I talked to Dunlop, and he said you could do your routine. He was impressed that a newspaper man would be here. So we have clear sailing. The minute the photographer comes in, I will give you a short intro and you will pop right up there, do your bit, and we will be on our way."

"Hey, Nutty," Orlando said, "smile pretty and look right into the camera."

Nutty didn't move. He felt pale, and all he could do was sit there and look at his meat loaf and green beans. Bilbo said, "Nutty, don't eat any of those beans or you'll barf for sure."

Nutty almost lost it all at that point. He pushed his tray as far away as he could, and then he put his head down on the table. "Take a deep breath," William said, "and then I want you to sit up and get your composure. Would you like a drink of water?"

Nutty sat up straight after a minute. He said he didn't need a drink. William kept telling him over and over that he didn't have to worry. Nuty mumbled a couple of times that he couldn't remember any of the jokes, but William said he would be right there to prompt him if it became necessary.

And then the photographer stuck his head in the door. He was a young guy with a droopy black mustache. Nutty said something. It sounded like, "Hraaaaa, aaaahhhh." William got up and walked over to the camera man, said something to him, and then he walked to the front of the cafeteria.

It was a lousy room for a comedy act. The long tables were arranged in rows. And since the seats did not turn, the kids had to twist around to see. But William marched right up to the front and yelled, "May I have your attention please? Students, please, may I have your attention?" The kids quieted down, but Nutty heard a six-grader at the next table ask who the little nurd was.

"As you are all aware," William went on, "we have in our school a wit of extraordinary skill, a humorist who will someday be a star. We have members of the press here today to hear what is usually given for your entertaiment alone. I give you the comedian who is a budding star . . . NUTTY NUTSELL!"

A big groan went up, and most of the kids turned back around in their seats. Someone yelled out, "You gotta be kidding," and some of the kids booed. Nutty got up and walked slowly to the front. He felt that he was on his death march. "This can't be happening to me," he thought to himself; "It must be some other guy named Nutty Nutsell." His heart was pounding, and he could only see a blur.

Nutty reached the front and turned to the audience. He gulped and then his mouth fell open, but nothing came out. He looked like a guppy. "Did you hear . . ." he started to say, but his voice pinched off and squeaked. Kids began to laugh, at least those who bothered to even look up. Nutty took a deep breath and pushed his hair back. The photographer came closer. Some of the kids must have been impressed by seeing the photographer because they began to quiet down again. This time Nutty almost yelled, trying to avoid another squeak, but now he sounded like a quarterback barking out signals. "Did you hear about the guy who went to McDonald's and got kissed by Ronald McDonald?"

"No Nutty, we didn't hear about that," some loud-mouthed sixth-grader yelled back.

"Well, see, it was all . . . a . . . a mistake. He . . . uh . . . or, I mean . . . they got it wrong. They thought he ordered a *big smack*."

"Was that a joke?" someone yelled. A few kids laughed a little, but a whole lot more just groaned.

Nutty took a quick breath and then let it out a little at a time. He could see that some of the teachers had gathered at the back of the room. They looked puzzled. Nutty hoped they weren't upset with him. "Yuh, well," Nutty went on, trying to laugh, the way William had told him to do, "that's better than what happened to the guy who crossed a jellyfish with a can of oil. You know what he got?" Nutty paused and counted to three, just as William had coached him to do. "He got petroleum jelly."

There were a few more laughs this time, but still plenty of groans. All the same, Nutty felt himself starting to relax. But then a flash went off. Nutty looked at the photographer and forgot everything. He stood there, his face all blank, and then he heard William whisper, "The elephant, the elephant."

"Oh, yeah," Nutty said—FLASH—"I mean . . . say, did you hear about the . . . oh, I mean, what do you call an elephant who walks through a Hostess cupcake bakery?"

"Oh what, Nutty, what?" Nutty decided to hate that kid.

"You really want to know, don't you?" Nutty said, and he was surprised when the kids laughed. All of a sudden he was almost comfortable. "Okay, then, I'll tell you what you call an elephant who walks through a Hostess cupcake bakery. You call him Twinkie Toes!"

This got a pretty good laugh, too, especially from the little kids. Nutty had thought all the jokes were stupid—he still thought so—and so he was relieved to get any laughs at all. Nutty saw the teachers shaking their heads and acting as if they were in pain, but they were smiling. Another flash went off, but Nutty was grinning and didn't care much any more. He remembered his next line. "Let me tell you about another guy—he was a strange fellow—he swallowed swords for a living. But he wouldn't swallow a sword without putting salt on the blade first. That was all right for a while, but he finally got thrown in jail." One, two, three. "Yuh, they got him for *a salt* with a deadly weapon."

Nutty couldn't believe what happened. The kids really laughed. No one booed or groaned or anything. It was a dumb joke and Nutty hadn't even wanted to tell it, but even old Dunlop was back there sort of chuckling and nodding. This was *all right*. "Well, folks, that's all for today," Nutty said, as he had been taught to do, "but let me give you one warning. Never stand up straight when boarding a helicopter. Now some might disagree—at least those who are more *open minded*."

Nutty gave a little bow—this was his own idea—and began to walk away. A few of the kids even gave him a little applause. And everyone was looking at him as though . . . he couldn't decide exactly what it was. It was as though he had done something important. As though *he* was important. Then a teacher yelled out, "Encore," and a few kids joined in. Nutty ignored it at first, but then he thought of another joke he knew and decided he might as well do it. He stopped and went back to the front. "Well, I *could* tell one more."

Nutty noticed that William was frowning at him, but he went ahead anyway. "See this guy . . . uh . . . was visiting at a—you know—an insane . . . uh . . . place. Whatever you call them. And see, this guy . . . no, wait a minute. Oh yeah, he sees this garden, see, and it's really a good one. So he says, 'How do you make your garden grow so well?' and the crazy guy says, or I mean, he asks the other guy, the one who was visiting the place, if he had a garden. And the guy says he did, and so then the crazy guy says, 'How do you make your strawberries grow so well?' I guess the guy had said he had good strawberries, or something. So the guy says, 'I put cow manure on 'em.' So then the crazy guy says, 'I thought we were supposed to be crazy in here. We put cream and sugar on our gardens,' or I mean, 'on our strawberries.'"

There was not even a chuckle, and then someone said, "That's an old one, but that's not how it goes."

Nutty walked back and sat down. He wished he could walk right out the door and straight down the street. Maybe even move to another neighborhood.

William got up. "Let's have a big hand for Nutty Nutsell. You'll be seeing him on *television* one of these days." Very few bothered to clap, but afterwards a couple of kids came by to tease. And Nutty's old third-grade teacher, Mrs. Price, came by as Nutty was getting up from the table. She told him she was very proud of him. Nutty just sort of nodded. He liked hearing her say it, but he knew he had been lousy, and he was sick about telling that last stupid joke. Still, there was something about all this that wasn't so bad. It was different from his usual goofing off. It was all sort of acceptable and even important, by comparison.

"Nutty, you were excellent," William was saying. "Honest. For a first performance you were better than I even hoped for. Your timing kept getting better and you relaxed. Honest, you were downright brilliant. But Nutty, don't ad lib. Not yet. I know the jokes are corny, but they are calculated for your K through six audience. That one you told is all right, but not suited. And you hadn't practiced it—and Nutty, it *was* rather an old one."

"I know. I blew it."

"Not really. Not at all. It was an excellent experience. Just don't branch out on your own too much. As long as you stayed with my material you were fine. Just trust me, Nutty. Don't make a move that I have not approved. Understand?"

"Yah. I understand."

CHAPTER FIVE

During the next few days, Nutty took a lot of teasing, especially after his picture came out in the newspaper. But he didn't mind as much as he would have before. Most of the kids who teased him sounded a little jealous. And besides, maybe he *did* want to become a comedian. He wouldn't have told anyone for anything, but he liked to imagine himself doing his first show on TV as the new "kid sensation." Or he pictured himself on talk shows: "Well, Johnny, I've come a long way since I first broke into this business."

Mrs. Smiley made a big deal out of the picture. She clipped it out of the paper and put it on the class bulletin board—the one with the cutout leaves that were already turning orange and red and gold. And after she talked about it, she said, "And I'm sure we all wish him well in his hopes of becoming a comedian."

It made Nutty feel good until Mindy turned

around and said, "He's not a comedian; he's just a joke." Marla, the girl who sat right in front of Nutty, laughed right out loud; but Nutty decided not to give them the satisfaction of seeing him get mad. He just sat there and gave Mindy a pleasant smile, and he didn't say anything at all. Probably Mindy was in agony because it wasn't *her* picture that had been in the paper. And there was something nice about just sitting there, watching her suffer.

"And you know," Mrs Smiley said, "I saw some more evidence of Frederick's talents in his essay. He wrote from the point of view of a fat old ape." Mindy's head popped around; she stared at Nutty in disbelief. Nutty knew what she was thinking. She had given him the idea. "The ape spends his life just lying around in a zoo, watching all the silly-looking humans who come around and stare into the cage. It was *very* funny. I laughed and laughed. Some of the people he described were so *very* funny."

"Did you look in the mirror?" Mindy whispered.

Nutty smiled at Mindy, but he didn't say a word. He didn't have to.

William called another meeting before the week was over. He claimed that the campaign was "turning the corner." But the major step, the "really crucial one," was Nutty's confrontation with Dr. Dunlop. The assembly was going to be on Monday. William said that he and Nutty would have to spend the whole weekend together, putting in long days of preparation. "That's all I need," Nutty thought to himself. "Ol' Father Time is coming to my house to play."

"But first," William said, "we must decide what our issue is to be. We must attack Dunlop where he is most vulnerable."

"Where he's what?" Richie asked.

"That means a weak spot," Bilbo said.

"That's right, Bilbo. We must find an issue that most students are concerned about, but it must also be an issue that strikes Dunlop where he has little defense. We cannot lose; if we do, we destroy Nutty's credibility."

"I didn't know he even had one," Orlando said, but William paid no attention.

"The point is," William went on, "you are going to have to tell me what the students are upset about. I am totally uninformed about that sort of thing."

"A lot of kids don't think they should have to pay fines for forgetting to bring back library books on time. Heck, they charge—"

"No, Orlando, that won't do. Precedent is too strong. Most schools do the same. And personally, I find the fines justified."

Bilbo said, "One thing that Dunlop has done is to cut the recesses down to fifteen minutes. Our old principal used to give us twenty minutes. A lot of kids don't like that."

"Well, Bilbo, that is more the sort of thing we need. But it sounds terribly childish and self-serving to ask for longer play periods. Isn't there anything else that students do not like?"

"The lunches," Nutty said.

"Hey, yah," Orlando said, "everybody hates the food they serve in the cafeteria."

"Well, I don't know," William said. "Personally, I have found the food to my liking so far. The meals are well-balanced, clearly nutritious and—"

"And taste terrible," Orlando said. "At the other schools in town the kids get hamburgers and hot dogs, pizza, all kinds of good stuff. Last year the student council asked if we could have stuff like that, and Dunlop said that it was junk food and he *would not* allow it." Orlando tried to imitate Dunlop's voice as he spoke the last phrase. The others laughed.

"Ah-ha," William said, and grinned his grandpa-grin. "Now I think we have something. I happened to come across a study that indicated that the hamburger does not make a bad lunch for young people when combined with other wholesome foods. Since the child is more likely to eat it, many nutritionists recommend it for school lunches in preference to more traditional school servings."

"My sentiments precisely," Nutty said, imitating William.

"Yes," said William. "And before this weekend is over, you will be an expert on the subject."

William spent most of the weekend at Nutty's house. In a way, that was all right with Nutty. His parents thought William was the greatest kid ever invented, and so they stayed away to let the two of them work when William came over. It was when William wasn't there that they drove Nutty crazy. With his mother it was: "Do you *really* think you have a chance to win, Freddy?" "What did Mrs. Smiley say about your picture?" "I called your grandmother in St. Louis—she was *so* thrilled. She said you're going to be just like your grandpa." And with Nutty's dad it was: "Son, a man has to go out and get what he wants out of life. No one hands it to him. I think you're starting to see that." "I remember when I ran for senior class president, back in my high school days. I lost that election by just a few votes. If I had it to do over again, I would go after it harder, campaign a little more, shake a few more hands. When you're young, you don't even realize what opportunities you are passing up." "Son, this is just the beginning."

Right, Mom. Right, Dad. Sure thing, folks. By the way, though, it's president of the school, not president of the universe. I'm in fifth grade, remember? It wasn't the kind of thing you could say. But you could think it—plenty. In fact, Nutty seriously considered getting a year younger on his next birthday and working backwards for a few years. Otherwise the whole trend would only get worse!

By the time Monday came around and the assembly was about to begin, Nutty felt like a hamburger patty himself. He had memorized an opening statement, and then he had learned a whole bunch of responses to things Dunlop might say. William had coached him on his delivery, enunciation, voice projection, hand movements, everything. And Nutty thought he had actually gotten pretty good, so long as he was standing up to William. But now he was scared stiff. He could see Dunlop up there with his big old jaws ready to start chomping down on him. There was no way he could pull this thing off. He tried not to think about it. Better to concentrate on his comedy career. Who needed politics when a guy could get rich telling jokes? "Did you hear about the nearsighted butterfly hunter who reached out and caught his bow tie in a mirror one day and almost broke his neck?" That was his own joke. Maybe he would need a writer.

Now Dunlop was asking whether any of the "pupils" had any questions, and William was nudging Nutty's ribs about halfway through his body. To his surprise Nutty found himself standing up. His heart was booming right out loud, and his vision was getting all blurry, "Yes, sir." He cleared his throat. "I mean, *yes, sir.*"

Nutty was in the middle of the fourth row, where William had told him to sit. Dr. Dunlop was straight ahead and above, on the stage, and behind the podium.

"Frederick Nutsell, did you have a question?"

"Yes, sir. Have you changed your mind about allowing contemporary foods for school lunch?" Nutty had tried to project his voice and had almost yelled. The words came out sounding memorized. He sounded like one of those really lousy actors in a school play.

"Allowing *what*?"

"Contemporary food, sir, For instance, hamburgers, hot dogs and pizza." William had chosen the vocabulary carefully. He knew the word "contemporary" would bother Dunlop. In fact, he hoped Dunlop would get flustered and angry and make a fool of himself.

"I believe, young man," Dunlop said, his head lowered so that he could see Nutty over his bifocals, "that most of the children understand that it is their own best interest I have in mind when I refuse to allow junk foods in the cafeteria."

Nutty was ready. William had guessed Dunlop's first response. Nutty's second speech went: "But, sir, have you done any research to determine whether contemporary foods do indeed lack nutritional value?" The room got very quiet. The kids had whispered and giggled when Nutty had first gotten up, but this was something new that he was doing, and everyone sat still, waiting for the explosion.

"Son," Dunlop said, trying to control his voice, "do you really think research is necessary in this case?"

"Yes, sir." Nutty let that jab sink in, and then he said, "Have you, by chance, seen the recent article in the *American Educators Journal*, under the title, 'Old-Fashioned Notions on Nutrition,' which argues that contemporary foods *should* be served in school lunch programs?" Nutty took a deep breath after getting those lines out. He knew he still sounded nervous, but he was picking up some confidence, delivering the lines with more sound of conviction.

"Who put you up to this, Frederick?" Dunlop

said. His voice was still under control, but it was on the edge of cracking.

"You did, sir. You asked if there were any questions." This was not one of William's lines, but Nutty's own, and Nutty thought he heard the sound of a harpoon—thwop—hitting Dunlop right in the chest.

Dunlop tried to think of something to say. Finally he blurted out, "You know what I mean." He was mad now. There was no mistake about that.

"Would you mind answering the question?" Nutty asked.

"What question?" Nutty could see the side of Dunlop's neck. It was the color of the sunset.

"Have you read the article?"

"No, I have *not*, Frederick. I will hear no more of this. We will talk about this after the assembly. Junk food is junk food, and *that* is *that*."

But this led Nutty right back into his memorized lines. "Actually, sir, noted nutritionists say that a fairly high carbohydrate lunch is not unhealthy for young people who lead active lives. When balanced with other wholesome foods, the contemporary entrée has the advantage of appeal. 'There is little advantage to good nutrition wasted on the garbage disposal,' one authority has stated." Nutty stopped while the kids were snickering. Dunlop had his hands on his hips and was glaring at Nutty—or was it at William? "Would you, Dr. Dunlop, in light of this information, reconsider? Would you at least read the article, which I have photocopied for your convenience?"

"Frederick, I have no intention to read—"

"You mean to say, sir, that you won't even *read* it? An article from the *American Educators Journal*?" This was not memorized. This was Nutty talking. And the words came out with intensity. No one moved.

Then Dunlop cleared his throat. "Now Frederick, you just control yourself. I certainly did not mean to imply that I would not read the article. I only meant that. . . ."

Nutty was on the move. He worked his way across the row of kids and then walked up the stairs and handed the article to Dunlop. There was no applause, just silence, but Nutty knew he had won a big victory.

"I make no promises," he heard Dunlop mutter.

Dunlop changed the subject after that, and he didn't ask for any more questions. He introduced some sixth grade kids who did a stupid skit about summer vacation being too long and everyone being happy to come back to school. Nutty paid no attention. He was thinking about the presidency—of the school for now. Then he would run for mayor, governor, senator, president of the United States. He was on his way. Why not president of the world?

As the kids filed out of the auditorium after the assembly, William kept telling Nutty he had been terrific. And kids were saying, "Way to go, Nutty."

As Nutty and William came out of the auditorium door, Jim Hobble and some of his friends were waiting. Hobble was big for his age and really mature-looking. He never wore jeans—just dressy slacks—and as he walked, he always looked around to see who was looking at him. But now he shot his hand out to Nutty. "Nice going, Nutty." And then he pulled Nutty off to one side. "Listen." He hesitated and let his head bob up and down a couple of times. "I could use someone like you. We could use you on the student council this year. Have you thought about running?"

"Not really."

"Give it some thought. Or ask your buddy William there to think about it for you. Doesn't he do your thinking?" Then he laughed and slapped Nutty on the shoulder. "Naw, just kidding. It took a lot of guts to do what you just did. Let's work together and see what we can get done this year, all right?"

Nutty found himself saying, "Okay," and even sort of liking Hobble's attention. But he couldn't stand the jerk. He wanted to beat Jim Hobble, and he wanted to beat him bad.

CHAPTER SIX

During the next few days Nutty's campaign began to look fairly strong. Of course, William was on top of everything. He saw to it that kids were chosen from each grade to lead the campaign in their own classes, and he instructed the kids on what to do. They were not to mention yet that Nutty was even running, just keep spreading the idea that someone ought to beat Jim Hobble. Of course, the kids were supposed to say good things about Nutty when they got a chance, but William told them not to overdo it. Then, just before the deadline, William would turn in Nutty's petition and the campaigners would come out in the open. All the organizing and instructing made the kids feel important, and they took their assignments very seriously. But of course, within a day or two some of them forgot their instructions and started promoting Nutty openly. But William said he had known that would happen. A few days of rumors would spread the word rapidly, and the timing was right.

William met with Nutty every day and told him what to do. Nutty was supposed to study harder than he ever had before, take part in class discussions, and act responsible—even intelligent, if he could. William even got Nutty to break up a fight during recess one day. Nutty felt stupid, but the fourth grade teacher, Mr. Julian, saw it and told Nutty he was proud of him. William thought that was great. He explained that it was important to spread the idea that Nutty was willing to stand up to Dunlop on a "point of honor," but no one should think of him as a troublemaker. His motives had to look right; he was trying to help the students and lead them, not just smart off to the principal.

But Nutty wasn't too sure about all this. "All those kids knew I was putting on an act," he told William. "And they hate it when a teacher says nice things like that about a guy in front of everyone. The kids will think I'm just playing up to the teachers."

"No, Nutty, that's not true. I'll explain." William took on his hands-behind-the-back-and-forehead-wrinkled-up-with-wisdom look. "You see, all voters know that a public figure puts on an act in order to win his office. It is expected. If the act is too extreme, it can backfire, but most people still feel safer about voting for someone who fits nicely into a prescribed image for the public office in question. Even though kids don't exactly like the 'school leader' type, they will vote for him—or her—rather than vote for a school troublemaker or a poor student. What's involved is more than popularity; people respond to a stereotyped image that fits a ready-made idea of what the public figure ought to be."

"William, I don't even understand what you're talking about."

"Okay, let me put it this way. Jim Hobble, in most ways, is the sort of child who wins these elections. He is confident and he is always the center of attention. Most kids don't really like him, but still they would have voted for him had we not entered the race. He has made the mistake of becoming too confident—cocky—and that is a quality kids don't like. What was needed, however, was a good alternative, and we have provided that. But you, as the new candidate, must still possess most of the qualities that kids associate with a student president. We have, I hope, erased some of your negative traits in their minds, and we are now replacing those with positive ones. Kids know that you are acting, but it is the act they expect—even demand—of their leaders."

"You mean they'll forget everything that happened last year?"

"Not entirely, of course. But people have short memories, and young people forget with amazing speed. I think they will buy this new image faster than you could ever imagine. Most kids probably didn't mind the firecracker incident. It won't really hurt you. In fact, it even fits in somewhat with your new image of fearlessness. But we have to make you look like a steady person, not just a flake."

Nutty could only stare at William. "William, is this how people get elected—I mean like for senator or for president—by putting on an act?"

"Well," William said with a big sigh, "you needn't put it quite that way. You simply package your product in the best possible wrapper, without really lying about the contents. We have told the public you are funny; you *are* funny. We have told them you are brave; you *are* brave. You stood up to Dunlop, didn't you?"

"Only because you told me to."

"But you did it, all the same. What's the difference?"

"A lot, William. I think there's a whole lot of difference." But when he thought about it, he wasn't exactly sure what the difference was, and the conversation ended.

Everything went according to plan for the next few days. William was predicting a landslide, and even Nutty was beginning to believe that kids were changing their attitudes toward him. But on the morning after the deadline for petitions, Dr. Dunlop dropped a bombshell. He gave his usual morning announcements over the intercom, but when he announced the candidates for student council president, he read off three names and not just two. Angela Vanghent, a sixth-grader, was the third candidate. William had been trying to pick up rumors of other candidates, but he hadn't heard a thing. Obviously at the last minute some friends of Angela's had decided to nominate her.

William spent the day finding out everything he could about her. From what he could gather, she was dependable, smart, well-liked, and she had served on the student council for three years. She was not shy, but she was not the Jim Hobble type either. All the kids William talked to said they liked her. Even the boys did.

At the end of the day, it was obvious to Nutty that William had begun to worry. He thought the whole situation over that night, and then he called a meeting the next day. The boys met that afternoon after school. William started out by giving his analysis of the election as things now stood. As he saw it, Angela was in a strong position. The boys would probably split their votes; but if most girls voted for Angela, she could win. Some boys might even see her as a better alternative to Hobble than Nutty, because she *was* a sixth-grader, and many still felt that the president should be in sixth grade. A "dramatic move" was going to be necessary now, William said.

"Like what?" Orlando wanted to know. The boys were sitting on the grass behind the school. William had his legs crossed under him, as though he were attempting a Yoga position.

"Well," William said, "that's just the question. I can give you some alternatives, but none is exactly attractive."

"But the kids won't vote for a *girl* will they?" Richie asked. "We've never had a girl president."

"Your question is an interesting one, Richie. Traditionally, females have tended to give little support to other females in elections. Men were almost more likely to vote for them than women were. But much has changed in recent years. Many women simply had the same image for the leader that men did: the supposedly strong, decisive, protective male. But now women—and girls—are beginning to say, 'We can do anything you fellows can do,' and unfortunately—or perhaps fortunately—they are right."

"*No way*," Richie said. "Girls aren't good at stuff like that."

"Evidence simply disagrees with you, Richie. Any educator or psychologist will tell you that most girls are more mature than boys at our age. So for this particular election, many girls would be preferable to most boys."

"Well, anyway," Bilbo said, "what are you going to do?"

"First of all," William answered, "we must hope that the school is full of bigots like Richie here. Maybe quite a few girls will hesitate to vote for one of their own sex, and we must hope that most of the boys will refuse to vote for a girl. Don't go around saying, 'Don't vote for a girl'; but you might drop the hint that a boy is probably preferable."

"Wait a minute," Nutty said. "You just said that girls were better."

"I only said they often are. But if there is a prevalent prejudice against females, we certainly don't want to talk kids out of it and cut our own throats, do we?"

Somehow, that didn't sound right. "William, I don't think it's fair to go around saying that kids ought to vote for me because I'm a boy, unless boys really are better."

"Wait a minute, Nutty. We aren't doing anything wrong. We're not saying that girls can't do the job; we're saying that boys make strong leaders. It's a cultural bias handed down to us for centuries. Why should we not use it to our advantage?"

"It's a what?"

"Never mind. The idea is to stress the strong, masculine leader image. You're tall, Nutty, and strong-looking. Your blond hair and suntan give you an athletic look—the 'team captain' image. Perhaps we can set Angela up in a situation that will cause her to appear rather weak, at least by comparison to you. I should be able to talk Dunlop into holding an assembly where the candidates are allowed to present their platforms. Hobble should come off rather badly at something like that—and further discredit himself. Nutty could stand firm, maybe present a new issue. We might have to resort to this longer recess issue, although I have misgivings about it. Angela is quite confident and will probably give a good talk, but if we can get Dunlop to allow questions, maybe we can challenge her to face up to Dunlop the way Nutty has. My guess is that she cannot do it."

"Yeah, a girl couldn't do that," Richie said.

"Richie, you are an amazing male chauvinist. Of course, some girls could, but only a few, just as only a few boys could. I'm just gambling that Angela won't. We know that Nutty *can* and *will*."

"But isn't that rather cruel, William?" Bilbo

asked. "I wouldn't want to get up there and have someone make me look scared, or stupid, in front of everyone."

"It depends on how you look at it, Bilbo. We are only bringing out her true colors. A leader must stand up under pressure. If she can do it, fine; we may be defeated. But if she cannot do it, she deserves to lose. I am trusting that we can get to her if we calculate the questions carefully."

Nutty had been listening but not saying anything. He was just rolling a blade of grass around in his fingertips, watching it spin. "William, isn't there some other way we could. . . ."

"I don't think so, Nutty. I have considered everything. We could try to find something in her records that would disqualify her, but that would be risky—getting her records, I mean—it could become our Watergate. Besides, chances are, she has nothing on her record to hide."

"That would be a rotten thing to do, anyway, William," Bilbo said.

"But it might be fun," Orlando said. "I always wanted to be a spy."

William ignored Orlando. "Well yes, Bilbo, it isn't the sort of thing I would like to do. But as to the pressure issue, that is the only thing, as I see it, we can do. We could try to make a deal with her, maybe offer her a chairmanship, or create a vice-president's office and offer her that. But she is in such a strong position she would be foolish to bargain. So I don't see any other options, or at least none that seems likely to work."

"William, I have an idea," Nutty said.

"Good. Let's have it."

Nutty leaned back and stretched his hands out behind him to prop himself up. In the last few days he had begun to think things through in ways he never had before. "Some kids are saying that maybe it would be better if Angela got it this year, because I could always run again next year. I think maybe that's right. If I asked all the kids who are going to vote for me to vote for her, she could win. As long as Hobble doesn't win, that would be okay with me."

"Nutty, a politician cannot think that way," William said, and he shook his stubby little finger at Nutty. "You must grasp the chance while it's there. Next year the world could be blown away for all you know. There is no next year—or should not be in *your* mind. If you are to succeed, you must believe you are the best, and you must act on that assumption."

Nutty just sat there and looked at William. He *did* want to be president. William had promised it to him so many times, it almost seemed his already, and he hated to give it up. And yet. . . . "But I don't want to—you know—do a bunch of rotten stuff. How would you like to be up there and have a bunch of guys trying to make you look like an idiot?"

"There, you see, Nutty, you *are* the strong, protective male. But I'll tell you what—if I were up there, I would accept the challenge. And should they make me look foolish, I would know I deserved to lose. You take the same chance she does, Nutty. Someone may try to discredit you. But you will be ready, and that is why you deserve the presidency. And don't worry about Angela. We won't push too hard; we don't want people to feel sorry for her. That could work in her favor. We simply need to demonstrate that she does not have your insight and foresight, your strength and courage."

"No—yours," Nutty mumbled.

"Excuse me? Did you say something?"

"Never mind."

CHAPTER SEVEN

When Nutty got home that afternoon, he stayed in his room for quite a while. He wanted to think about the election and what William had been saying. But he couldn't really decide anything. Finally he went out and found his sister in the family room watching cartoons on television. She was sitting on the floor.

"Susie," Nutty said, "could I talk to you?" She didn't move. Her eyes were zeroed in on the TV. "Hey Goldilocks—I said I wanted to talk to you."

Susie turned around, halfway, still sitting on the floor. "What do you want?" she said. Then she turned back to the television set.

"Could you turn that thing off for a minute? I want to ask you something, all right?"

"Are you serious?" she said, not even turning around this time.

"Yah. Come on," he said. He walked over and

punched the off button, and Tom and Jerry faded into green nothingness. Nutty turned around and looked at his sister. She was holding a hairbrush in her hand and had apparently been brushing her hair just before Nutty had come in.

"Susie, is anyone in the third grade going to vote for me?"

"I don't know."

"Don't you ask them?"

"No."

"Why not?"

"Why should I?"

"Because I'm your brother."

"Yah, but I don't want *them* to know that."

"Come on, Susie, lay off." Nutty was standing in front of her with his hands on his hips. He had on his faded jeans with a tear in the knee and an old T-shirt that was too small for him.

"Well . . . . would you want anyone to know that you were *your* brother if you were me?"

"Lay off. They all know I'm your brother. Now give me a serious answer before I stick that hairbrush of yours in the toilet."

"Oh, yuck, Nutty—you think of the worst—"

"Susie, just answer. Is anyone in the third grade voting for me?"

"I *told* you, I *don't* know. Some of the boys prob'ly will. Sean and Douglas are supposed to be your campaign guys or something, so I guess they will. I don't know."

"What about the girls? What do they say?"

"Amber thinks you're cute."

"Come on, Susie."

"They don't say anything. They don't care who wins. Marjie says she's voting for Angela 'cause she's a girl. She's the only one who even says anything."

Nutty sat down on the floor in front of Susan. "What about you?" She didn't say anything. She started brushing her hair. "Well, are you going to vote for me?"

"I don't know. I want to watch TV, okay?"

"Do you think I could be a good president?"

"Yes."

"Do you really, Susie?"

"Yah. President of the weirdos!"

"Thank you," Nutty said. "I can't tell you how much this little talk has meant to me." Suddenly he reached out and grabbed her hairbrush. He jumped up and ran out of the room with it. Susie chased after him, but Nutty turned and went into the bathroom. When she got to the bathroom, he was holding the brush over the toilet. He had it between his fingers and was letting it swing back and forth, as if it would drop at any second.

"Please, Nutty, don't," Susie said. "Come on. I was just kidding."

Nutty just kept holding the brush where it was. "Would you like to join my club? It's for weirdos—you should fit right in."

"Come on, Nutty."

"Ah—you don't want to be in my club. I guess I'll just. . . ."

"Oh please don't, Nutty. I'll join."

"Are you weird enough?"

"Yes. Come on."

"Good. You're the new president." Nutty handed the brush to her and walked past her, down the hallway to his room. He sat on his bed for a while—just sat there. After a few minutes he picked up his football and gripped it as though he were going to pass it. He pulled the ball back to his ear and pretended he was passing for a touchdown. He watched the pass receiver break into the open, and then he fired the ball to him. The receiver caught it over his shoulder without even breaking stride. Six points. Nutty sat on his bed and listened to the crowd cheer. "I must be going nuts," he thought to himself. "I ought to know better than to ask that little twerp something like that." In a few minutes he got up and went to the phone in the kitchen. He called Bilbo.

"Hello. Bilbo?"

"Yah."

"You wanna throw a football around or something?"

There was a long pause. "I guess not."

"Why not?"

"I don't know. I got started reading something that I want to finish."

Nutty hesitated. "You really get into that stuff, don't you?"

"Well, yah. It's really good though, Nutty. You'd like it. It's Ray Bradbury. Have you ever heard of him?"

"Yah. From you." There was another pause. "Bilbo, what do you think about all this stuff?"

"You mean the election?"

"Yah." Nutty slid onto one of the stools near the phone at the kitchen counter. He leaned over and rested one elbow on the countertop and rested his cheek on his hand.

"Well, Nutty, I don't know. I sort of wish that William had never come to our school."

"Me, too," Nutty said. "Or I wish he would leave. Maybe he'll retire. I think he's about due to get his pension, isn't he?" Nutty could hear Bilbo's deep-voiced Hobbit chuckle. "But what about this stuff with trying to make Angela look bad and smarting off to Dunlop?"

"That's what I mean, Nutty. I'd just rather get back to—you know—normal."

"But do you think it's bad to do that stuff?"

"Well, yah. I think it probably is." Nutty sat up straight. "In this one book I read this guy. . . ."

"Are you sure, Bilbo? I mean, should I just get out of the whole thing?"

"I don't know, Nutty. Maybe so."

"Bilbo, do you think I would be—" Nutty stopped. "I mean, would I be okay for a president?"

The silence really bugged Nutty. Finally Bilbo said, "Well, the whole thing is—it's not like it's really an important thing. William is the one that makes it sound that way. But I guess anyone could do it."

"Even me, huh?"

"I just mean. . . ."

"I know. But could I do it as well as Angela?"

"Maybe after you got started. You could learn about running meetings and that kind of stuff."

"So maybe I ought to run for student council this year—and let Angela win. Then next year—after I've had a little experience—I could run for president."

"Yah, I guess. William would say. . . ."

"I don't care what William says. I'm tired of listening to William. I'm going to get out of this whole mess. I'm going to go see Dunlop in the morning and tell him I'm withdrawing. Don't you think I should?"

"I guess so, Nutty. I mean, I guess that's what I would do, but. . . ." Nutty wasn't listening any longer. He had twisted around to see his mom and dad behind him. He didn't know how long they had been there. They were in the opening between the living room and the dining room, and they each had a grocery sack; they were both staring at Nutty as though he had just called home to say he was in jail.

"Bilbo, I've got to go." Nutty hung up the phone and turned around on the stool. His parents were still staring at him.

"Freddy," his dad said, "you can't be serious."

"I was *talking to Bilbo*—I didn't know you were listening. . . ."

"Oh son," Mrs. Nutsell said, "you can't do this. You just can't. I called your grandmother, and I told all the—"

"Now that's not the point, Linda," Mr. Nutsell said. "It's a matter of being a fighter or a quitter. When things get tough, a man finds out what he's made of. Freddy, no son of mine is going to back down the first time the competition gets a little tough."

"That's not it, Dad. That has nothing to do with it." Nutty got up and walked toward the kitchen door.

"Freddy, come back here," his mother said. "We've got to talk about this."

"I'm going over to Orlando's."

"Now wait just a minute, son," Mr. Nutsell said. "You are not going anywhere until we have talked this out." Nutty stood where he was, near the door. "I have been very proud of you these last few days, Freddy. You have been showing me that you have some of that old Nutsell drive in you. I just can't let you drop out of this election. You'll be sorry for it the rest of your life."

"Okay."

"Okay, what?" Mr. Nutsell finally set down the sack of groceries and came around to the other side of the counter, closer to Nutty.

"Okay. I won't drop out of the election."

"Just like that?"

"That's what you said to do."

"Well, yes. Fine. But . . . just like that?"

"Oh, Freddie, what's the trouble?" his mother asked. "Are you afraid of losing? You don't have to be afraid of that. We would never feel bad about that. Is that the trouble?"

"No. I'm afraid of winning."

Mr. Nutsell nodded his head a couple of times, and then he seemed to relax. He undid his tie. "Ah . . . now I understand. Well, son, everyone has gone through that. It's lonely at the top. There's no question about that. But don't let it get to you. A leader of men has to—"

"Dad, some of the stuff William is doing is not right. We're cheating."

"Cheating? What do you mean?"

"William writes out everything I say. And he makes me pretend that I'm some kind of hot shot. And he wants to get Angela up there in an assembly and then ask her a lot of hard questions and make her look stupid. I don't think that's right."

"Well, is *that* the only problem? That's politics, son. That's just the way things are."

"Okay."

"Okay, what?"

"I'll run if you want me to." Mostly Nutty just wanted to get out of the conversation. "I'm going over to Orlando's."

"Freddy," his mom said, "we have company coming for dinner and you—"

"Who's Orlando?" Mr. Nutsell asked.

"Jimmy."

"Since when did you start calling him that?"

"Since William told us to. William does all our thinking for us." Nutty headed out the kitchen door and down the hall.

But his dad came into the hallway before he could get away. "Son, we'll talk some more about all this. We'll get this all settled. Just don't do anything silly like . . . Freddy, don't be gone very long."

Nutty got his bike out of the garage and blasted

down the street as fast as he could go. If there was no getting out of the election, there was no getting out. That was all. "It could be worse," he said to himself. "At least I still have a good chance of losing."

Orlando only lived a couple of blocks away; Nutty pumped hard and was there in no time. He felt like playing football or racing someone. And he wanted to win. He was glad when he got to Orlando's and saw that Richie and Orlando were out in the driveway shooting baskets.

"Hey, Nutty," Orlando said, "come on and play."

Nutty set his bike against the side of the house and said, "All right. I'll play you both."

"Okay," Orlando said. He was standing near the rickety old basketball standard, holding the ball. He had on his Kansas City Royals baseball cap. Orlando threw Nutty the ball, but then he turned to Richie and said, "I'll cover Nutty, and you play back for the re-bound."

Orlando charged forward, but Nutty dribbled right past him. When Richie tried to head him off, Nutty pulled up and took a jump shot. He missed the shot, but he was taller than either of the others and he was able to grab the rebound and put another shot up. This time he got the basket. The whole game went that way; Nutty won without any trouble. Orlando was a fairly good shooter; but if he missed, Nutty had the rebound every time. Richie wasn't very good at all. When he took a shot, Nutty just went for the rebound. He knew Richie would miss. Nutty beat them twenty to eight. They played twice more, but he beat them just as bad both times. After the third game the boys were sweating in the sticky heat. They walked over to the shade of the house and took a rest.

"Hey, Nutty, you're pretty good," Richie said. Nutty knew that Richie always thought everyone was better than he was—at everything.

"I'm not good. I'm just tall."

"That's true," Orlando said, grinning. "If I were as big as you, I'd beat you easy."

"That's probably right," Nutty said. "But I didn't cheat or anything, did I? I mean, I can't help it if I'm bigger."

"What's the matter?" Orlando asked.

"Nothing. Why?"

"How come you said that?" Orlando actually seemed serious for once.

"No reason," Nutty said. "I'm just not very good. I play with this kid from junior high sometimes. He wipes me out."

"You'll never be any good if you talk that way." Orlando took his cap off and wiped the sweat from his forehead, then flipped his black hair out of his eyes and put the cap back on. "My dad says if I'm going to make it to the majors, I've got to think positive."

Nutty sat down on the driveway and leaned against the house. "What'll you do, Orlando, if you don't make it in baseball? Is there anything else you would—"

"Dad says to never even think of that. He always wanted to play in the majors—when he was a kid growing up down in Texas—but he says he didn't stick to it. Now he's sorry because he was really good."

Richie said, "Yah, but it's hard to make it, isn't it? My dad always says you should try hard, but if you aren't good enough, it's not your fault."

"I'm good enough," Orlando said. He got into his batter's stance. "You ever see me hit?" Orlando concentrated and then he took a hard swing with his fists held together as though he were gripping a bat.

Nutty was thinking that lots of kids were good, but that it was not so simple to make it all the way to the majors. He didn't say it though. He didn't feel like putting Orlando down. Maybe something *was* wrong. Putting Orlando down was his favorite pastime.

"What would your dad say if you told him you didn't want to play baseball?" Nutty asked.

"He'd kill me," Orlando said, and then he took another cut with the imaginary bat.

"No. I mean really?"

"I don't know. We just always talk about me playing. It's what we both want."

"What if you change your mind?"

"I won't," Orlando said. "I'm too good." He grinned, and then he mashed a fastball that sailed out of the park.

Nutty wondered. He was getting to think he understood some things, but he couldn't tell anyone exactly what they were.

"Hey, Orlando," he finally said, "that was strike three."

"No way. That was a homer."

"Then how come the ball is in the catcher's mitt?"

"What are you talking about? Here comes the kid who caught it in the stands. He wants me to sign it for him."

Nutty just laughed. He turned to Richie. "What are you going to be?" he asked.

"Are you okay?" Richie said.

"What's wrong with you guys? How come you keep asking me that?"

Richie was leaning against the house, with his legs crossed at the ankles and his fingertips stuck in his jeans' pockets. Nutty looked up, but he had to wait for a while before Richie would answer. "I don't know. You never asked me anything like that before."

"Like what?"

"Like what I want to be."

"Okay, so now I am. What do you want to be?"

"Well, I don't know. I was talking to my dad last time he had me for a weekend, and—"

"Are your mom and dad divorced?"

"Yah."

"You never told me that before."

"I know. I don't usually say too much about it. And you never asked me or anything."

"Is it kind of weird—I mean, just seeing him on weekends like that?"

"Yah, in a way. At least it was at first. I'm kind of used to it now. But anyway, my dad said I shouldn't worry about what I want to be yet. He said I should just wait and see what I'm good at or what I like when I get older."

"You'll never be good at anything if you do that,"
Orlando said. "That's what my dad says. You gotta
start young and go after what you want."

Nutty got up. He looked at Richie. Richie always
seemed sort of unimportant. His ears stuck out, and
one of his front teeth had come in sort of sideways.
And he always looked down if you looked right at
him. "Richie," Nutty said, "sometime—like when you
spend a weekend with your dad—could I maybe meet
him?"

"My *dad*?"

"Yah."

"I guess so."

"All right. I've got to go, you guys." Nutty walked
over and got his bike. "Hey Orlando, you gotta stay
alive out there. You just let that pop fly drop right in
front of you." Then Nutty got on his bike and took
off. He was almost home before he remembered that
his mom had said that company was coming for dinner. That was the last thing he wanted. He really had
to talk to his father one more time: he really did want
to get out of that election. Maybe if he explained it
right, his dad would understand.

A car that Nutty didn't recognize was in the
driveway. He wondered who was there. As soon as he
got inside, he looked in the living room and there was
William sitting in the big chair that Dad usually sat in.
And on the couch next to him was a pudgy little man
who looked exactly like William. The pipe in the
man's mouth was the only difference. Next to the
plump little man was a plump little woman who was

wearing a sweater—a wool sweater. The temperature was at least eighty outside, and she was wearing a sweater.

"Oh, there you are," Dad said. "I just called Jimmy's to see when you were coming home. I had a chance to meet Mr. Bilks today—I stopped by his office. I thought it was about time we got to know William's parents, since you two have become such good friends."

Mr. Bilks stood up. He was not much taller than Nutty. He thrust out his hand, exactly the way William always did. "So this is the young man I've been hearing about. William tells me you are to be the next school president. Congratulations."

Nutty shook hands with him. "Thank you," he said.

CHAPTER EIGHT

There was no point in trying to resist. He had to go ahead and run. And being forced into it did at least save him the trouble of making a decision for himself.

William was able to arrange the assembly he had talked about. Dunlop agreed to let the candidates give speeches and answer questions. Nutty was not surprised; he was not surprised by anything William did any more. But Nutty was not happy about the evenings that would be spent memorizing his speech and then practicing it over and over with William for an audience. William said that every possible question had to be considered so that Nutty wouldn't be caught in the trap that was being set for Angela.

At least there were a few days before it had to happen. The assembly was going to be just two days before the election. William was busy following up with campaign workers, trying to find out how the "voting trends" (as he called them) were going. Hobble seemed to be disappearing from the race. All the kids, except a few sixth grade boys, said they were planning to vote against him. But Angela was looking stronger all the time. Almost all the girls in the school were promising to vote for *their* candidate—and there were more girls than boys in the school. Most of the boys were backing Nutty, but some would probably vote for Angela because she was a sixth-grader, whether they admitted it to the other boys or not. Still, Nutty had become a sort of hero to a lot of kids because of his brave stand before Dr. Dunlop. William said that Nutty had a good chance, but Nutty could see that most of William's confidence was gone.

It took a while but eventually Jim Hobble seemed to catch on to what was happening. At first he couldn't imagine that he could be beaten by either a fifth-grader or a girl, but then he began to hear too much talk not to realize that most kids were not voting for him. One day at lunch he came up to William and Nutty at the lunch table.

"Hey guys, can I talk with yuh for a minute?" Nutty thought he sounded like the used car salesman who had once tried to sell his dad a '66 Corvair.

"Sure," Nutty said. Jim sat down next to Nutty; William was on Nutty's other side. Orlando, Richie and Bilbo were on the opposite side of the table.

"Listen, I want to tell you guys that you are running a great campaign—no kidding." He said "you guys," but he looked right at William, leaning out to look around Nutty. "The only thing is, the way things

are going, I'm afraid we're going to split the boys' vote
and Angela is going to win. I really hate to see a girl
win, if you know what I mean."

"Why?" Nutty asked.

"Why what?"

"Why do you hate to see a girl win—if you know
what you mean?"

"Don't get cute, Nutsell," Hobble said, but then
he seemed to catch himself. "What I mean, Nutty, is
that you could be president next year, but this is my
last chance. Why should we let a girl take it away from
us?"

"You mean, 'away from *you*,'" Orlando said, grinning.

"Look, you guys—I don't know what you're trying to pull." Hobble was trying to control his temper,
you could tell, but his voice was getting shaky. "I
should think you would hate to see a *girl* win this
thing."

"Why?" Nutty asked again.

"What are you talking about? We guys have to
stick together, don't we?"

"Why?" Nutty asked. Hobble just stared at Nutty,
as if he was some kind of freak. "I mean, since when
did you ever stick with *us* on anything, Hobble?"

"Yeah," Bilbo said. "You never lowered yourself
to speak to us before."

Hobble looked around at each of them. He was
getting downright ticked off, and Nutty could tell it.
All the guys, except William, were grinning. "Look,

Bilks, you understand this kind of stuff. Don't you hate to see the guys split the vote and let a girl get in?"

William put down his fork and seemed to think for a second or two. "I have no objections to a girl as president. Surely, no one today believes in those old myths of male superiority. In this particular case, Angela strikes me as a much better choice than you. No offense intended, of course—but you asked. Angela, on the whole, seems brighter than you, more organized, more capable of leadership, and she is not arrogant, as you are. As to loyalty to a fellow male, simply because he is a male—that strikes me as illogical, and in fact, stupid. By that logic, I would have to support any fool who ever ran for office—including yourself—just because we share the same gender."

Hobble spoke in a low voice, but he was getting hot. "You little *toad*. You're the one who came in here and messed up everything. Nutty doesn't have the brains or guts to do any of this stuff. I would have won *easy* if you hadn't goofed everything up for me."

"You may have won, Hobble," William said. "You may well have. But since you are not going to win now, why don't you withdraw? It would save you some embarrassment, for one thing. And if you are so dead set on seeing a boy win, withdraw and give your support to Nutty, a male and a winner."

"Not a chance, *Bilks*. I'd rather see a girl win than a stupid fifth-grader."

"My, my, such bigotry," William said. "But then you seem to have little attachment to anyone—except, of course, yourself."

Hobble reached for William, but he reached in front of Nutty, and Nutty grabbed his arm. "Lay off, Hobble. Why don't you just take off now."

Hobble wrestled his arm forward and then slammed his elbow back into Nutty's chest. The blow knocked Nutty right off his seat. He sat on the floor sort of stunned for a minute, and then he bent forward and grabbed his chest. Hobble looked confused. He might have been afraid that he had hit Nutty too hard. But then Orlando yelled, "What did you do that for?" Everyone in the cafeteria was looking now. William was down checking Nutty. "Well, why did you?" Orlando yelled again. "You think you can push everyone around, don't you?"

"Shut up," Hobble said.

"Don't you know that's why no one will vote for you?"

Suddenly Hobble grabbed Nutty's tray and threw it at Orlando. Orlando ducked, and the tray flew over his shoulder and slammed against the wall. Mashed potatoes and corn stuck to the green paint for a second and then slithered down to the floor.

Teachers were coming now, but William had hold of Hobble. He had gripped the tendon in Hobble's shoulder, near the neck. Hobble sank to his knees, struggling to get free at first, but then starting to beg, "Let go. Please. Oh, please, let go."

"Let him go," Mr. Julian said. William did. Julian grabbed Hobble's arm and led him from the cafeteria, while all the kids stood and watched. Another teacher was helping Nutty to his feet.

Within ten minutes the principal had called in several kids to give their accounts of what had happened. Before the day was over, everyone was saying that Nutty had tried to stop Hobble from beating up William. And of course, they were telling the story of Wiliam's death grip on Hobble. But the story was still good for Nutty's image. He had stood up to Jim Hobble—a sixth-grader.

By late afternoon the word was getting around, too, that Dunlop had suspended Hobble from school for three days and disqualified him from running for president. It was a great boost to Nutty's chances.

Nutty was not completely happy about the whole thing, however. He had hoped to beat Hobble in the election, not have it happen by default. But William was loving every minute of it. "It was just the break we needed, Nutty. We have a good chance now. Things were really beginning to look bad."

"I guess so, William. But I hate to win by just getting lucky."

"What do you mean, lucky?" William said. "Why do you think I kept insulting him? I knew he was getting ready to do something stupid. We just showed him up for what he really is. And you acted the part of the hero you have now become. That wasn't luck. You actually were trying to defend me. Maybe Orlando's anger was a bit of good fortune, but over all, I merely forced a situation that gave everyone a chance to see that you are the better person. You came out well, but only because you are a natural defender of the little man."

Nutty rolled his eyes. "The 'little man' seemed to handle himself all right."

"I did rather bring him down, didn't I?" William said, smiling a bit, looking like a proud old fellow who had just won a game of chess. "By the way, how are you feeling? Did he hurt you?"

"I'm okay."

"See, it all turned out perfectly. It couldn't have been better if I had planned it that way."

CHAPTER NINE

Now that the election only involved two candidates, William was a whole lot happier. Most girls were still lining up behind Angela; but William felt Nutty's chances were not bad—the assembly would be the key. Dunlop almost crossed everything up, however. He was upset by all the trouble with Hobble, and he threatened to cancel the assembly altogether. William talked to him, though, and was able to get a fifteen-minute assembly that would be held in place of afternoon recess. The speakers would only get five minutes, and two minutes would be allowed for questions. Dunlop called Nutty and Angela in ahead of time and held a ceremonial coin flip to see who would speak first. And then he told both of them, "I am tired of this whole business. We have never had such a fuss before over these elections. Let's have no trouble today—of any kind. And keep your talks to the five-minute limit."

Nutty and Angela agreed, of course. Nutty would gladly have cut his talk much shorter, or not have talked at all. But his talk was ready and had been timed. It lasted about three minutes. Most of the kids were mad about missing recess for the assembly, and they would be in no mood for long talks. William hoped that Angela would go on and on and hurt her chances that way. Nutty was going to be "to the point, and precise."

Dunlop got up first that afternoon and gave a little speech about the "American way" and freedom to vote, while the kids whispered and paid no attention. Nutty and Angela were sitting on the stage behind Dunlop. "We had a flip of the coin to decide who would go first," Dunlop said, as he was finishing up. "We wanted to be fair, in every way. So in this case, the lady will *not* go first, but Frederick Nutsell will."

Nutty walked to the podium. A microphone was staring him in the face. He cleared his throat and heard the sound, like a growl, bounce around in the auditorium. That kind of scared him for a second. He gulped, but then he smiled the way William had told him to do, and he took a deep breath. It was getting to be almost natural to smile so unnaturally.

"My fellow students. The story is told of a farmer whose horse was sick. One day he asked his neighbor, 'Say, John, didn't you have a sick horse awhile back?' 'Shore did,' John answered. 'Well, what did you give him for it?' John replied, 'I gave him a gallon of gasoline.' And so the farmer decided to try the same remedy on his own horse, but the next morning he found that his horse was dead. So when the farmer saw his neighbor again, he said, 'Say, John, didn't you tell me you gave your horse a gallon of gasoline when it was sick?' 'Shore did,' John answered. 'Well,' the farmer said, 'I tried the same thing and my horse up and died on me.' 'Yup,' John said. 'So did mine.'"

Nobody laughed very much, but Nutty counted to three as he waited, and then he went on. "Perhaps you have been given such advice at some time—advice that seems good but that just doesn't work out. I know I have been hearing lots of advice about this election. Many are saying that boys ought to vote for a boy; others will tell you that if you are a girl, you ought to vote for a girl, that girls ought to stick together. . . ." Some of the girls in the audience gave a little cheer. For a moment Nutty lost his train of thought, but he recovered quickly. Two weeks before he would have just caved in if something like that had happened. "But students, it is silly to vote for such childish reasons. If we do, we make the whole election meaningless. We may be young but we have rights, and we have our own opinions. Vote for someone who is ready to fight for your rights and to turn your opinions into policies."

William and the other fifth-grade boys began to applaud, and a lot of the kids joined in. Nutty waited, as planned, and then said, "Thank you; I am glad you agree—glad to know that we are grown up enough not only to vote, but to vote for the right reasons. You will remember that at our last assembly I raised some serious questions about the food served by our cafeteria. So far, Dr. Dunlop has chosen to give no answer to my questions, but if I am elected, I will pursue this issue until we do have answers—until we have better food."

William started the applause again. Nutty then reminded the kids of some of his former arguments for "contemporary food." Dunlop didn't move; he just stared toward the crowd.

"But now another issue needs our attention. Our recesses have been drastically reduced, and our recess is the first thing to be cancelled when our schedule has to be adjusted for a day. Educational psychologists unitedly proclaim the need for young students to combine healthy exercise with daily academic training. The issue is not merely for more playing time, but for our health and emotional well being. As your president I will fight for reversal of this dangerous trend." Kids were clapping this time, and William didn't have to start it. Dunlop was like a statue.

"So let me say in closing that the president of this school needs courage and conviction, and he should be a person who is willing to represent the students' rights. No longer should our president serve as a mere puppet to the administration. A government *of* the people and *for* the people—that is what we need, and that is what I will work for if you elect me."

A lot of the boys in the crowd had been coached to jump to their feet and cheer at this point. Almost all the boys in the auditorium joined in. But what surprised Nutty was that quite a few of the girls stood up, too. Were they crazy? They had to know that he couldn't do any of that stuff! Dunlop was going to grind him up and sprinkle him on the shrubs outside for fertilizer. He'd be blowing around like dust when Dunlop got finished pounding on him. There was nothing to do but sit down.

"Boys and girls," Dunlop said, with a very stern voice, "this whole thing has gotten out of hand. The child who has been elected as our president has always . . . how shall I say? . . . simply presided at student council. And the student council only talks about school parties and that sort of thing. I don't want you children to get it in your heads that you can run the school. That simply is not the way things are done. Now I think you all know this. And I know you will all remember it when you vote. I wouldn't want to try to influence the vote, but I hope you don't think that any such tactics will be allowed here. I've never had anything get quite so out of . . . well, never mind. Our next speaker is Angela Vanghent, one of our nicest sixth-graders." He turned to leave, and then came back. "Did you want to ask Nutty, or I mean Frederick, any questions?" And without hesitating at all, he said, "Fine. Go ahead, Angela."

Angela stepped up on a stool behind the podium so that she could see, and then she looked down at her paper and read her speech. "Boys and girls, I am happy to be a nominee for the office of student council president. I consider this nomination a great honor. Since I was on student council last year and for two years before that, I believe I have the experience to serve as your president. If you elect me, I promise to do the best job I can."

That was it. Nutty was embarrassed; that speech was about what he would have come up with had William not written his for him. And it was a better talk than his own had been—it seemed to fit the situation better. The girls in the audience were clapping, but not very hard. Most of the boys didn't clap at all. But Nutty did.

Angela came back to her seat near Nutty. She had dressed up special for the assembly—in a light blue dress with a white collar—and her long hair was held back with a white ribbon. Nutty thought she looked nice. She *was* nice. He really didn't know her very well, and he had no special feelings for her—but she was no snob or nurd or anything. It crossed his mind again that it would probably be better if she got elected.

"Hi, I'm Nutty Nutsell," he said to himself. "I'm made out of wood. The funny little old guy you see is the one who sticks his hand in my back and makes my mouth move. Watch his lips very carefully, and you might catch him talking for me."

Dunlop then asked whether anyone had any questions for Angela. Several seconds went by, and Nutty hoped that William would leave her alone. But then a sixth-grade girl raised her hand.

Dunlop motioned, and Angela went back to the podium. "If you are elected president, will you also try to get better lunches and longer recesses?" The girl sounded as if she were out of breath.

Angela didn't say anything for a long time. Nutty watched her from behind and wondered what she was thinking. He even hoped she would give a good answer. In fact, he wanted to jump up and say, "Hey kids, don't expect her to do things that I couldn't do either. I'm just a wooden dummy. Look at my back and you'll see the place where William sticks his hand in to make me talk." But he didn't say anything. He just sat there and hated himself.

"I would," Angela began, and then cleared her throat. "I would talk to Dr. Dunlop about the lunches. But I think fifteen minutes is probably enough for recesses."

There was no applause. And there were no other questions. Nutty couldn't believe that Angela would be crazy enough to say such a thing. All the same, he liked her for doing it. Angela sat down, and the assembly was dismissed with a little time still left for recess.

"Angela," Nutty said, "I . . . a. . . ."

"It looks like you're going to win, Nutty," she said. "How did you ever think up such a good talk?"

"I didn't," he mumbled, but he didn't explain. Didn't she know? Didn't everyone know by now? "You gave a good talk," he said. "Better than mine."

She laughed. "Nutty, you *are* a politician."

"No, I mean it," he said.

She laughed and then walked away. Nutty wanted to run after her and tell her again that he was serious, but he didn't. William was waiting at the foot of the stairs when Nutty came down from the stage. "Perfect, Nutty. We should have the election wrapped up now."

"I don't know. Don't you think that kids will catch on that I'm just saying what you tell me to? I think they. . . ."

"Nonsense. All politicians have writers. It's your charisma that makes the speeches so effective."

"My what?"

"Your style—your personality. You're great, Nutty. Just believe that, and you will be all right."

"How come you guys didn't ask Angela any questions?"

"I hit on something better. I happened to be talking to Brenda—the girl who asked the question—and she was asking me a little about campaigning. I guess she's a friend of Angela's. I told her I didn't mind giving her a few tips, and said that her candidate needed to show more forcefulness, come out more clearly on the issues. I told her she might ask Angela in the questioning period whether she too would fight for student causes."

"You set her up, William. That was rotten."

"Not at all. It was perfect. No one could claim that we tried to harass the other candidate, and yet what I told her was actually good advice. Angela did need to take a stronger stand. I simply gambled that she wouldn't be willing to take that stand. And—as it turned out—I was right."

"But, William," Nutty said. He stopped and

turned toward William. "She didn't lose her cool the way you said she would. She gave a good answer."

"She gave the wrong answer."

"But it took guts to say what she said."

"Oh yes," William said. "She's quite a person; I agree. I was impressed with her courage. I even agree with her about recesses. Nonetheless, it was the wrong answer, and it should cost her the election."

"Wait a minute, William." William had turned to walk away, but Nutty caught him by the arm and turned him back around. "What do you mean, you agree with her?"

"I just think fifteen minutes is long enough for a recess. Our studies are much more important. Kids get plenty of playing time after school."

"Well, then, why did you have me say that?"

"Because it's an issue that most kids can identify with. Who doesn't like recess? A politician has to find issues that the average person can easily understand and rather automatically agree with. The *real* issues will only appear after you win. You can't do anything for the students until you have the office."

"I don't think that's right, William. I don't even get what you're talking about. I need to think about all this."

"No, Nutty, don't think. Just trust me. I've brought you this far, haven't I?"

CHAPTER TEN

Nutty did spend a lot of time thinking that night. When he stayed in his room after dinner, his dad came down the hall and poked his head in the door. "Hi, son. You working on your victory speech?" He laughed and then stepped into the room. "Listen, Freddie, your mom and I were just talking, and we just want you to know that you don't have to feel that you have to win to make us proud. We're proud of you, win or lose. You've shown us that you have some of that old Nutsell spunk. That's what counts."

"Okay."

"Okay, what?"

"Just okay." Nutty shrugged. What did his dad want him to say? What do you say when you're told you have Nutsell spunk?

Mr. Nutsell came over and sat down on the bed next to Nutty. "You know, son, holding an office is holding the public trust. Have you ever thought of it that way?"

"No." He didn't even know what "the public trust" was, but he knew better than to ask. His dad would probably tell him.

"Well, it is. It's representing the people. It's caring more about them than about yourself." He took a long pause while he let his head nod a couple of times. "You just might have a future in politics, son. Who knows? But if you decide to go in that direction, I want you always to be honest. Honesty is what's got me where I am today in sales." When Nutty didn't say anything, his dad said, "Will you always remember that?"

"Yah."

"All right. Well, I won't make any more speeches. You probably want to be alone on this of all evenings."

Mr. Nutsell left. Nutty had his answer. He was going to withdraw. That was it. He was going to show his dad what Nutsell spunk was all about—and throw in a little honesty to boot. All the same, he would withdraw first and tell his dad afterwards.

The next morning Nutty had an announcement for William: "I've decided to drop out of the election and let Angela have it. I think she would do a much better job, and I'm just tired of this whole mess. You and I both know that Angela will be a whole lot better president than me."

"Than I."

"What?"

"Than I. Correct grammar is 'better than I.'"

They were standing in front of the school, on the steps. Nutty had understood William's words, but not his reaction.

"Well, don't you. . . ."

"Don't I want to beg you to reconsider? Is that what you want? I will run through my arguments again and see if I can change your mind, if that's what you really want."

"No I just. . . ."

"You just thought I would be shocked. But I am not. Many great leaders—or great potential leaders— lose their nerve. Most people are content to be sheep and let others herd them. It doesn't surprise me that you are frightened and feel the temptation simply to step back into the herd."

"That's not it, William." Sometimes when William got that oh-how-wise-I-am look on his little round face, Nutty wanted to pug his nose a little bit more, but he knew better than to try that. "I don't know whether anything I say is right. I don't know if it's me talking or you."

"*I* or you."

"Okay, William. *I* or you. But I don't think *I* am running for president. *You* are running *me*."

"Every candidate has a campaign manager."

"Not in an elementary school, William. I'm in fifth grade, remember?"

"What's the difference, Nutty? The concept is still the same."

"I don't know, William. I don't think so. You get

me all mixed up. But I do know that Angela would be a better president than either *me* or *I*."

"Yes, in one sense, you are probably right about that."

"What?"

"Well, isn't that what you are asking for? Honesty?"

"Sure, but how come you keep pushing me if she's better?"

"Now listen, Nutty. This will be our last conversation on this subject. The fact is, right now she is better prepared than you are. She seems more mature, more self-controlled, and more experienced in student government. But the fact is, the president of this little school has never really done anything, and she won't either. The office is only for a pretense of democracy. Our campaign has raised the issue of student rights—giving the kids a voice in setting school policies—and you have become the leader of that movement. Two weeks ago you were the school goof-off; now you are about to rise above your own past. You can step back from that if you want to. I certainly don't care if you do. I have delivered on my promises. You decide whether you want to be the old Nutty or the new one."

He let Nutty think about that for a few seconds, and then he said, "This afternoon I have a little rally planned. We are going to be handing out 'Nutty Buddy' ice cream bars, wrapped in paper with 'Nutty for President' printed on the outside. Your father was nice enough to say he didn't mind paying for the ice cream. The plan is to get the kids gathered around by giving out the ice cream bars and then have you give a little impromptu speech. I have a couple of jokes and a little talk written out for you; you take it. Now if you would prefer to announce your withdrawal instead, you do that. You have all day to think about it."

William opened his briefcase and got out a sheet of paper. A couple of jokes and a few lines of a speech were typed out—nice and neat. He turned then and went into the school.

Once again Nutty had a hard time concentrating on his school work. Mrs. Smiley had the kids working on an essay called, "My Favorite Flower." Nutty could only think of a rose and a pansy, and he didn't want to write about either one. He finally decided to write on dandelions, just to see if he could make her mad. But she came by and saw what he was doing and said, "Oh my, Frederick, you have the most wonderful ideas!" Then she whispered in his ear, "By the way, good luck in the elections tomorrow. I hope you win."

"Thanks," he said, at the same time glancing over to see Mindy giving him an evil eye. As soon as Mrs. Smiley walked away, he said, "Hey Mindy, if you need any help with your paper, I'll be glad to give you a hand."

"That's not even cute," Mindy said. "The only thing I want from you is for you to keep your big mouth—"

"Mindy, let's turn around now and do our work," Mrs. Smiley said.

"It was Nutty who started it, Mrs. Smiley. He told me that if I—"

"Never mind. Let's just do our own work." Mindy shot Nutty one more sour glance, but she didn't dare say anything else. Orlando was cracking up—he had to put his head down to keep from laughing. Even William was smiling. But Nutty didn't really care. He was still trying to remember what he had decided the night before—and why—and he tried to think about what William had said. But he really couldn't make much sense of anything.

By afternoon, however, he had reached a decision. He would withdraw from the election—not because of any arguments, but because he was tired of thinking about the whole thing. He felt better immediately. All this presidency stuff didn't really interest him anyway. He would go outside and tell the kids, and then he would go tell Dunlop, or better yet, Dunlop's secretary. Then he would go over to Orlando's or Bilbo's and throw a football around or something. "Nutty for President" even sounded stupid. How had he ever let William get him into all this? "This dummy will now speak for himself. I quit—and get your little fat fingers out of my back."

As he walked outside, he was feeling a whole lot better. But then a bunch of the guys started screaming, "Yea, Nutty. Yea, Nutty. Nutty for PRESIDENT!" William and Orlando were handing out ice cream bars, and kids had gathered around in a big gang.

"Here's your new president," Orlando yelled. "Give him a big cheer." The kids all started to yell.

Half the kids were girls, and even they were cheering him.

"Let's hear a few words from Nutty," William yelled above the noise.

"Yeah, speech, speech," someone yelled, and other kids picked it up. "Speech, speech, speech."

William led Nutty to the front of the crowd. Nutty turned around and looked at everyone. He couldn't remember what he was going to say. He hadn't even looked at the jokes or the talk William had prepared, so he couldn't use that stuff. But the kids were getting quiet, so he had to say something.

"Uh . . . I have been thinking about the election and everything, and . . . uh . . . well. You know. I'm not exactly sure . . . in a way . . . whether I can really . . . you know . . . do it."

"Sure you can," Orlando yelled.

"You can get us longer recesses," someone yelled. "If anyone can do it, you can, Nutty."

"Yuh, well I . . . don't know . . . I. . . ."

"Nutty stood up to Dunlop," another kid yelled. "No one ever did that before." The kids cheered.

Suddenly Nutty liked it. He liked it a lot. He had never been a hero before. "Well, anyway . . . did you ever hear about the near-sighted butterfly catcher who caught his own bow-tie in a mirror and almost broke his neck?"

The kids laughed as though he had actually said something funny. Nutty couldn't believe it. Maybe it was funny.

"Well, I just wanted to say that if I'm elected I'll

do my very best. And I'll try to keep the pressure on old Dumb-lop."

The crowd laughed and cheered, and then more kids crowded in to get their ice cream bars. Others were beginning to leave. A couple of kids slapped Nutty on the back and told him he had it in the bag. But as Nutty walked back into the school to pick up his homework, he saw two teachers talking seriously and looking at Nutty. Nutty guessed that they weren't very excited about the ice cream bars. How was he going to deal with people like that—teachers, and Dunlop? William was simply going to have to do most of it for him. As long as he had William, maybe he could manage. But he really wished—or at least part of him wished—that William had just run for president himself.

CHAPTER ELEVEN

The next morning all the kids voted. At about ten o'clock Dr. Dunlop came to the fifth grade room and asked Mrs. Smiley if he could see "Frederick." As Nutty walked out the door behind Dunlop, William gave him a nod, and Richie said, "I'll bet you won. He's going to tell you."

Nutty followed Dunlop all the way to his office, and sat down when Dunlop motioned for him to. Dunlop sat down behind his desk, and then in a stern voice, as though he were announcing a suspension or a death in the family, said, "Frederick, you have won the election."

Nutty nodded, but he was not exactly thrilled.

"I feel that I must set something straight right now. William Bilks, needless to say, is behind all this. I don't think you would have taken the course you have taken had he not led you into it. Fortunately, however,

106

I have met with William and his father this week, and we have come to the mutual agreement that an elementary school—at least this one—is not right for Mr. Bilks, or that is, William. They are considering a school for the mentally gifted, or something of that ·sort. In any case, William will be gone soon."

Nutty felt as if somebody had just hit him in the stomach—hard. This was the worst thing that could possibly happen.

"Now, Frederick, it is unfortunate that this whole election got so out of hand. With William leaving, I believe we can get things back to normal, however. You will preside over the student council, and that is your entire duty. Do you understand that?"

"Yes, sir."

"I don't mind telling you, Frederick, that I think it is improper to have a fifth-grader as president. I think I will do something to see that this never happens again, but for now we will let it go. Angela Vanghent, in my mind, would have been a very nice choice. And the Hobble boy has always been a fine young man. I don't know what got into him this time. Had William Bilks not . . . but that is neither here nor there. The point is that you have won, and won by making a great many silly promises. I can't reverse the election—or at least I won't—but I can tell you that you might as well forget all those William Bilks ideas right now. Is that understood?"

"Yes, sir." Nutty was beginning to feel sick.

"The student council will deal with school parties, holiday programs—that sort of thing. Is that also understood?"

"Yes, sir."

"Now, Mrs. Smiley tells me your work has improved greatly over the past week or so. I hope Bilks is not doing your work for you."

"No, sir."

"Well, that is a good sign. Perhaps all this attention has been good for you in a way. Mrs. Smiley feels that you are a bright young man and that you are just beginning to live up to your true capabilities. You just might be a good president once you are on your own and are not influenced by a troublemaker. Do you think so?"

Nutty didn't say anything. He avoided Dunlop's eyes, but he could feel them zeroing in on him like laser beams.

"Well, do you think you can settle down now and be a good president, or are you lost for words when you have no one to write your speeches for you?"

"I don't know, sir . . . I. . . ."

"Well, that will do. This doesn't have to turn out badly. If you will simply quit allowing William to do all your thinking for you, I believe we can work together. You can go back to your classroom now. I'll announce to everyone, later in the day, that you have won."

Nutty thanked Dr. Dunlop and got up from his chair. Dunlop didn't even look up as Nutty disappeared out the door. Angela was sitting in the outer office. Nutty nodded to her as he walked by; then he stopped. "Angela, he's going to tell you I won. I'm sorry."

"I don't really care," she said. "I knew you would win." But she blushed and looked down at the floor; maybe she cared more than she wanted to admit.

"You know about student council and everything, don't you? I mean you've been on it quite awhile. Do you think you could help me?"

"Sure," she said. "I guess so."

"I mean, I know that sounds like what Hobble would say, or William, but I mean . . . I really don't know what I'm doing. I'm going to need help from the kids who do."

"Okay," she said, looking sort of puzzled. "I'll help if you want me to. But it's not a big thing. We don't really do much anyway."

"That's good," Nutty said. "That's what I'm good at: not doing anything." Nutty thanked Angela and then walked back to class; but when he got there, he went directly to Mrs. Smiley and asked for permission to speak to William in the hall.

"Well, all right," she whispered. "Just for a minute. Did you win?"

"Yah," Nutty said; but he let it go at that. There were more important things to think about than the election now.

William went out in the hall with Nutty. They closed the door and then faced each other. William leaned against the wall and slid his hands into his front pockets.

"Well, you won, I assume."

"Dunlop told me you're leaving. Why didn't you tell me?"

"I didn't want to upset you. I didn't want to do anything that might interfere with your campaign."

"You mean *your* campaign."

"*Our* campaign for *your* election."

"No, William. It was your election. You won. You proved to yourself that you could make *anyone* president. What am I supposed to do now? How am I supposed to be president without you? You told me everything to say and everything to do to get elected, and now you're going to take off."

"That will be better for you, Nutty. You'll have to do it on your own, and you will."

"I guess I'll do something. I'm not sure what. But that's not the point, William. What we did was wrong. You made up some guy and told everybody it was me."

"What?"

"I'm not like that, William, and you know it. We lied to everyone. And now I'm stuck with being some guy you invented! Everyone's going to know pretty soon that I don't know what the heck I'm doing. I'd beat you up if I could, but I can't even do that."

"Nutty, two weeks ago you had no confidence in yourself at all. Now you're telling *me* off. You're starting to realize who it is that you can be."

"William, you're missing the whole point. We *cheated*. We told lies so that I could win."

"What lies?"

"You know what lies. We said I was going to be a comedian, for one thing."

"Aren't you?"

"I don't know. I doubt it."

"Well, you can if you want to be. You have always been good at making people laugh."

"But we made it sound like . . . I don't know . . . like I already was, or something. What about all that stuff I'm supposed to do? The lunches and the recesses and all that?"

"Aren't you going to do them?"

"No, William. I don't know how. I mean, I'll try, I guess, but. . . ."

"That's all you promised to do."

"But you even said that you don't think longer recesses would be better."

"But that's my opinion. You have to consider what the people want. You represent *them*."

"William, stop it. STOP IT! You can't just keep making things right by turning words around. You . . . William, it's time you started to grow up."

"What?" William stood up straight and stared, but Nutty stared right back. "What did you say?"

"That's right, William. You heard me. You play around with people like they're toys—but you don't take any responsibility for it. It's just a game to you. You don't care about me. You don't care about anyone—except yourself. You're just like Hobble. You want to be a big shot, I guess. You like to run things just to be running them, and you don't care at all if you're messing people up."

"Nutty, I think you are—"

"Shut up for a minute, William. Listen to some-one else for once in your life. You came in here a cou-ple of weeks ago and told us you were going to win our friendship by doing stuff for us. You promised us trips to Chicago and everything else. You think you can just buy people off that way. You're smart, so it's easy for you to get things—and it's cheap for you to give the stuff you can get. But you haven't won *my* friendship. I'm glad you're leaving. I wish you had never come here."

William wasn't standing up very straight any-more. He was leaning back against the wall and look-ing more like a kid than Nutty had ever seen him look. As he stared into space, it was obvious that he was thinking.

Nutty let him think for some time, and then he said, "William, I don't want to be too—"

"No, that's all right, Nutty. Don't take it back. I just need to think about what you have said to me." William turned and leaned his back against the wall and stared across the hallway. Nutty felt embarrassed, but he didn't say anything. He let William concen-trate. Finally William said, "You've given me some harsh criticism, Nutty. I am going to spend much more time thinking this all through. You accuse me of being Machiavellian, and I suspect there is something to that. Perhaps my motives have been a bit more al-truistic than you give me credit for, but—"

"William, I don't understand what you're—"

"Well—sorry about that—I simply mean that I accept your assessment of me. I think my intentions have been somewhat better than you give me credit for, but I cannot deny that I find pleasure in manipulating those around me. In my defense, I can only say that I have been given more power than most ten-year-olds ever possess, and I think anyone would be tempted to misuse such power. I actually use more self-control than you might imagine. All the same, you are essentially right, Nutty. You are a bright person, and you have good instincts. You will be a fine president."

"William, that just isn't true. I just talked to Dunlop, and he backed me right against the wall and dared me to fight back. I was saying, 'Yes, sir, no, sir, whatever you think, sir.' I started waving my white flag before he even aimed a gun at me."

"If I were you, Nutty, I would—"

"Lay off, William. Don't get me into trouble again."

"No, I guess that's right. You better handle this your own way. You can be the kind of president the school has always had, the kind Dr. Dunlop wants. It's for you to decide."

"Oh wow, William, you just never stop, do you?" Nutty said. "Look, I can't face up to Dunlop. I get scared and can't think what to say. There's just no way that I—"

"Fine, Nutty. I understand. You have eaten those lunches all these years. Why not a couple more? Right? So what if you told the kids you were going to keep the pressure on? They will just figure you have reverted to your old self, and forget the whole thing. They may claim that you have no nerve without me there to back you up, but then, I guess you can live that down."

"William, lay off, please. You're just trying to push me all over again. I'm not getting back into that."

"Excuse me, Nutty. You're right. I was starting my manipulations again. I will leave you alone. You were a hero for a few days—and I think you enjoyed it—but in some ways being a nobody is a lot more comfortable. Of course, I suppose if you do nothing at all, that does make both of us liars, just as you suggest."

Nutty shook his head in disgust, but there was a faint smile beginning to show up on his face. William was in the middle of one of his full-scale, double-barrel, ninety-year-old-grandpa grins. "I'll always hate myself if I don't do anything, won't I William?" Nutty said.

"Well, I really cannot say, Nutty. That is for you to judge." But he was still grinning that all-knowing grin of his.

Suddenly Nutty spun around and headed down the hallway. William went waddling after him, but he couldn't keep up. Nutty marched right past the secretary and directly into Dr. Dunlop's office. He stopped and waited; Dunlop finally raised his balding head, and then he looked at Nutty with only a very slight sign of surprise. "Dr. Dunlop, excuse me," Nutty said. "I need to talk to you for just a minute or two."

"Yes, Frederick, what is it?"

"Did you ever get that article read?"

"Article?"

"The one on 'contemporary foods.'"

"Now wait just a minute. I thought we had an understanding about this. You said you were going to be no problem."

"I'm not trying to be a problem. But there are some things I've got to do. I just don't see why we can't have lunches we like better—especially since the other schools in town don't seem to think it's such a bad idea."

"Listen, Frederick. I am the principal of this school. I will not have the children trying to take over and tell me—"

"No one is trying to take anything over. But we have a right to tell you what we think. We have a right to look things up and make suggestions. And I don't see that it hurts for you to listen."

"I *always* listen. But I'll have no more talk on this junk food business. And I'll have no more of your disrespect."

"Disrespect? You're the one who shows no respect. You haven't even read that article, have you?"

"I glanced through it, Nutty—or Frederick. But I have no intention of giving way to this sort of pressure."

"Dr. Dunlop, I haven't used any pressure. All I did was ask you to read one little article. I guess we could put some pressure on you. I've thought about going over to see the president of the university, or writing letters to the town paper. Some of our parents agree with the kids, and I could try to get them to go to—"

"Now Nutty, let's not get carried away. I have not taken the time *yet* to read the article, but I certainly plan to. I have never said that I would not give the matter some thought."

"That's good, sir. I don't see why we can't work this out. Could I stop by tomorrow, or the day after that? After you read the article we could—you know—have a talk about it."

"Fine. We'll do that. But I don't like this William Bilks routine. I'm sure he put you up to this, told you every word to say."

"No, sir. That's not true. I'm talking for myself."

"Well, fine. I suppose. I still don't like the thought of . . . but I suppose it would do no harm for us to talk about it . . . just so long as you don't . . . you know . . . start writing letters and all that sort of thing."

"I think it would be much better if we could work it out together, Dr. Dunlop." Nutty was grinning a very wise grin—he couldn't help himself. "Would the day after tomorrow be all right then?"

"Well, all right. You come by, and we'll . . . talk . . . at least we'll *talk*. I make no promises, you understand."

"That's okay. I'll see you in a couple of days. Thanks, Dr. Dunlop." Nutty left. But he found that William was out in the hallway waiting.

"What happened?" he asked Nutty.

"I'm not sure," Nutty said. "You weren't standing behind me, were you?"

"No, I was out here."

"You didn't reach in and stick your hand in my back and make my mouth move, did you?"

"No, Nutty, I didn't," William said. He was grinning again.

"Well then, I guess I just 'initiated a series of high-level negotiations.'"

"You sound like a politician, Nutty. Maybe you better go into politics instead of comedy."

"I think I'll do both," Nutty said, and William chuckled and said something about the two being more or less the same. Then William stuck out his fat little hand, and he and Nutty had themselves a good handshake.

ABOUT THE AUTHOR

DEAN HUGHES grew up in Ogden, Utah, where he attended Weber State College. He received his Ph.D. in English from the University of Washington and completed postdoctoral seminars at Stanford and Yale. Since 1972 he has taught English at Central Missouri State University.

Mr. Hughes has published scholarly works on Charles Dickens and William Godwin and has written two adult novels, *Under the Same Stars* and *As Wide as the River*, which recount the story of the Mormon expulsion from Missouri in the 1830s. He also writes nonsense verse, which has been published in children's magazines and anthologies.

He is married to Kathleen Hurst Hughes, who is a special education teacher. His children, Tom, Amy, and Robert, serve as his advisors and critics for all his writing.

WITTY ADVENTURES BY
FLORENCE PARRY HEIDE books

☐ **BANANA TWIST**   15258/$2.25

Jonah D. Krock and Goober Grube are not the best of friends. In fact, they're not friends at all. But funny things can happen that turn an uneasy rivalry into a wacky friendship.

☐ **BANANA BLITZ**   15258/$2.25

Jonah D. Krock can hardly wait to get to the Fairlee School, which boasts a TV and a refrigerator *in every room*! But Jonah's in for a surprise when his "new roommate turns out to be his old arch-rival Goober Grube!

☐ **TIME FLIES!**   15370/$2.50

Noah is not looking forward to the birth of the new baby; he is convinced that babies only cry and scream and dribble— and they never help with the chores! But when the baby accidentally brings a $200.00 prize, Noah decides the baby isn't so bad after all.

If laughs are what you're looking for—check these out.

☐ **15366 ALVIN FERNALD, T.V. ANCHORMAN**
by Clifford B. Hicks $2.25
Alvin Fernald, 12-year-old possessor of the Magnificent Brain, proves that kids can do it better—on T.V.!

☐ **15211 THE WACKY WORLD OF ALVIN FERNALD**
by Clifford B. Hicks $1.95
In five truly nutty adventures Alvin Fernald uses his Magnificent Brain to bring about some surprising results.

☐ **15381 C.L.U.T.Z.**
by Marilyn Z. Wilkes $2.25
Meet C.L.U.T.Z. the second-hand robot whose housekeeping bloopers are driving the Pentax family bonkers.

☐ **15395 ME AND THE WEIRDOS**
by Jane Sutton $2.25
What do you do when your whole family's weird, *really* weird? You try to unweird them, of course.

These books are available wherever Bantam Books are sold. Or order today.